I0518788

THE LOVING MANY

by

Robbie Moffat

PALM TREE PUBLISHING

PALM TREE PUBLISHING
Paisley, Scotland Pa1 1TJ

© Robbie Moffat 2014-2019

First published in paperback JANUARY 2019

Typeset: Verdana 10pt

ISBN-10: 0 907282 76 8
ISBN-13: 9780907282761

PREFACE

Love and romance, action and adventure, the ingredients of good story telling. What the writer fails to tell us, we have to fill in for ourselves.

And so it is with The Loving Many, we take up where the story left The Loving Few in another age, in a gone-world of yesteryear, when there was war and plague everywhere, and relationships were cut-short by death, illness and madness.

DEDICATION

This book is dedicated to Pat Trevor.
Rest in peace.

Violence is the art of bullies
the trade of traders in ideas ...
it does not determine who is right;
victory goes to those who survive.

PART ONE

1

The Olympics were over; the band in the Piccadilly grill was playing the hit of the season *Shine on Harvest Moon*. There was a buzz, but it was all men's talk about cricket, motorcars, and politics. It was not the sort of conversation that interested a fifteen-year-old girl.

Everyone at Roedean had been talking about the Pankhurst's and the cause of women's suffrage. In support they wore little sashes of purple, green and white, and before the end of term, Olive had joined a group of the older girls to go up to London for the two hundred thousand strong demonstrations at Hyde Park. Jostled by the police and men hostile to the idea of women being granted the right to vote and stand as members of Parliament, Olive had become decidedly militant and headstrong about the rights of women. Accordingly, as she sat in the blue and gold decorated Grill with a long gold cigarette holder smoking a Passing Cloud cigarette that she detested, she thought about what a wonderful world it would be if women ran it. For too long men had put women down. Well, she was not going to stand for that in her lifetime. No man would ever get the better of her.

She blew the smoke slowly up into the air. She wished that her school-chum Jane Cooper would hurry up and get off the dance-floor. All the while, cocking half an ear to the Palm Court Orchestra, she could see a well-dressed man who could not take his eyes off her. Every time she looked in his direction, he made eyes at her in a way that could not be mistaken for anything less than flirtatious. He made her feel quite tingly, but she did not encourage him. Time and time again she looked away, but always, her curiosity would make her look in his direction again, until at last, encouraged by this, he approached her.

The prospect of having to deal with the advances of a man frightened Olive to death. From the corner of her eye she saw him confidently cross the room. At first she thought that he might keep walking and pass by her and that he would be swallowed up in the Grill crowd and never be seen again, but she was mistaken. She perceivably blushed when he came to a halt three feet from her. She felt so embarrassed, she did not dare to lower her eyes from the ceiling, and took a long inhale of cigarette.

"You're Olive Trainor aren't you?" he asked in an effeminate voice as he took a seat beside her. He was immaculately dressed in a dark Savile Row suit that looked almost new. There was not a crease on it, there were no wrinkles at the back of the jacket where the wearer had lounged in it; his trouser creases were the sharpest she had seen in her life. He was clean-shaven, round faced, and had lost most of his hair. At close range he seemed rather fatherly, and if there was one point that she did not like about him, it was the fact that he must have been more than twice her age.

Olive broke down into a fit of coughing. Someone had recognised her? How could that be, she was not even old enough to be a debulante yet. The coughing would not go away.

"My goodness let me get you some water." He snapped his fingers and a waiter came running on the double, took his order, and returned almost instantly with a tall glass of water with a twist of lemon. Olive sipped the water.

"Filthy things those" he motioned with a pointing finger at her cigarette. "Do you think you should ruin your health with such stuff?"

Olive, despite her own dislike of cigarettes, was not going to be told what to do by a man who was old enough to be her father but who was not. She put the cigarette holder once more to her lips, inhaled lightly, and blew the smoke in his face.

"Have we met before?" she said curtly.

At that moment there was sudden frenzy of activity in the Piccadilly Grill. There was loud clapping and a bunching of people around the doorway. Then, with amazing orderliness, the crowd parted with bows and curtseys and into the centre of the Grill appeared the most famous man in England followed by a bevy of young women.

"Look, it's the King!" someone declared close-by and everyone rose to their feet.

Edward was sixty-five, bulbous, bloated and debauched. His role as monarch had not diminished his appetite for the company of beautiful women. The government had long given up worrying about the King's wayward behaviour and scandal just seemed to improve his popularity with the average man. Women on the whole disapproved of his conduct and had great sympathy for the long-suffering Alexandria who had put up with her husband's adulterous behaviour for over forty years. As far as Olive was concerned, from the stories she had heard at Roedean, King Edward was a dirty old man.

This point of view was re-affirmed when Olive set eyes on the King. He was pop-eyed with an atrocious moustache and a beard, out of which stuck a cigar. He seemed to wobble, and if he did not have two women on each arm, Olive thought he would surely fall over like Humpty-Dumpy. He was a disgrace. How could such a man be King of England? Was it not a fact that the best monarchs England had ever had were both women? Virginity and chastity seemed the virtues for greatness, not lechery and profligacy. He was not a great king, he was not even a great man, and he used his position like some decadent Roman emperor who gave parties while his Empire declined. That much Olive had learned at school about Empires - they came and they went, not by a process of fate, but by bad management.

Then, to Olive's shock and horror, she recognised one of the women on the King's arm. It was her sister Chloe! How could she?

Chloe for her part had also seen her sister. As the King's party began to mingle with the other Grill guests, Chloe crossed the room and in a rage of temper sent Olive's cigarette holder flying out of her hand. It fell to the floor and skittered behind a palm. "Don't you ever let me catch you doing that again!" Without another word, she spun on her heels, and fled back to the side of 'Bertie' who had not even noticed she had gone.

Chloe had become the family's black sheep. Against the wishes of Marion and Patrick, on her 'coming out' she had gone on the stage, taking the name Chloe O'Hara. Almost instantly, through some other Roedean girls, she had fallen in with the 'Bertie' set. She was frequently invited to stay with the daughter of the Crown Equerry at Windsor. At first, Marion, not wishing to lose contact with her daughter, consented, but later, after hearing the gossip, threw Chloe out of the house. Initially Marion had thought that by entering into such company close to the royal household, Chloe would get noticed by the Queen, not the King. The Queen had any number of nephews and grandsons, and it was possible that the beautiful dark looks of Chloe might turn one of their heads. After all, rubbing shoulders with royalty was not new to Marion's side of the family.

Edward as king had moved the entire court back to London and the Palace of St. James's and Chloe had already been formally introduced to the Queen's great-grandsons Edward and George, next in succession after their father, Edward's son George. But they were mere boys, and

Chloe, every inch a woman, and every inch noticed by men, quickly found herself courted by the King's friends, and then the King himself. She willy-nilly threw herself, so to speak, on to his arm. This involved intimate moments that we will not enter upon in detail here.

The manner of entertainments Chloe provided for a man almost fifty years her senior must be left to the imagination, but it must be conjectured that the beautiful soft-skinned body of a gorgeous eighteen year old girl passing itself along the whale-like torso of an obese old age pensioner with skin like an elephant's, must lead many readers to the conclusion that power corrupts, and that wealth buys beauty in order to defile it. This of course may not always be the case; the young and beautiful may also learn from the old and ugly, and in return for sexual favours, may have the reward of mental endowment. Perhaps, like some poet eternally seeking a beautiful woman as the muse for his next love poem, King Edward sought inspiration for his next stroke of diplomacy from the likes of Chloe O'Hara. If we are romantics then we might accept this, but if on the other hand we are righteous and moral, such an argument clearly demonstrates the King's depravity.

Let us recall that the King had lost his virginity to Chloe O'Hara's grandmother. Does it not seem incestuous and as barbaric as some West African potentate for a King of England to have sexual intercourse with the third generation of his first conquest? Perhaps this is how royalty has spawned itself for millenniums, breeding with its own offspring. In this case we can be thankful in the knowledge that Chloe O'Hara was not the King's own grand-daughter, but who can safely say that one or other of the other young debutantes he bedded, without his knowledge, was not a direct descendant.

Within minutes of his appearance in the Piccadilly Grill, King Edward had moved on with his entourage to some other society venue. Olive never saw Chloe again, except on two occasions, once on the cover of Vanity Fair with a head of curls like the silent-movie sweetheart Mary Pickford; and for the last time, laid out in a coffin at her funeral. She had contracted diabetes like her grandmother Olive and been given a few months to live. Not content to go out with a whimper, she booked the Piccadilly Grill and threw a party for her set (later paid for by her mother) which included a lavish banquet and untold crates of champagne. Chloe drank herself into a coma out of which she never re-emerged. She died the following afternoon. The cortège was thronged with mourners, and it was the attendance at the chapel of all of Chloe's set that made Marion and Patrick realise that their daughter had been well liked and that they had made a mistake by disowning her. By then it was too late, but they failed to learn from it, as we shall hear later.

In the meanwhile, the man who had recognised Olive and had received smoke in his face as a consequence, now stood with a broad grin as he watched her search amongst the palms for her gold cigarette holder.

"Don't just stand there!" she bleated, "Help me. Jane Cooper will kill me if I do not return her mother's precious ciggy stick."

The man did not move. "You are not a bit like your mother" he said and walked off with a laugh, leaving her on her hands and knees in the palms.

"Olive!" declared a fresh faced young girl with a young man on her arm. "What are you doing?"

"Jane ...you won't believe it! I've lost the ciggy stick." Amongst friends, Olive dropped the precise diction she had learned in Brooky's schoolroom and at Roedean.

"Oh, get up, Ollie, mother has hundreds of them."

"But it was gold, Janey."

"Don't be silly. Mummy can't afford real gold since Daddy divorced her." She flicked back her beautiful head of blonde hair. She looked like an Amazon; she was tall, blue-eyed and athletic, the best tennis and hockey player at the school for her age. She was also the eldest of three sisters who were related to the Duke of Rutland. "By the way, who was that man?"

"God knows" Olive replied. It was a puzzle to her, but she said it in such a way as to suggest that she knew more than she was letting on.

"That was one of the Fletcher twins, darling" the young man said "Don't ask me which one. They're identical."

"Oh ..." Olive knew exactly who the Fletchers were. Their father had cheated her mother out of Notting Hill. Some years earlier he had convinced her to sell it to him at a knock down price. He had subsequently leased the land to speculators who built rows of town houses in imitation of Kensington who paid him an annual rental that far exceeded the purchase price. George Cramm, a solicitor who worked in Fletcher's legal department was friendly with her sister Cecily and told her of the goings on. Marion was furious. She had always trusted James Fletcher, though Alice James had warned her to be on her guard with him. George Cramm, after further research, found that Fletcher had also bought the foreign investments that had come with Marion's inheritance for practically nothing, when in fact they were of considerable value. Patrick insisted that she took Fletcher to court for swindling her, but Marion did not want to risk the rest of what was left of her fortune on financing a legal battle that she might not win. She did not want to die penniless. With careful and prudent management, she could maintain Patrick and the family as a well-off upper middle-class unit.

Olive did not know the ins and outs of the Fletcher swindle, but she vowed that if she ever met a Fletcher, she would not be nice to him. She felt angry that she had missed her opportunity, but she mentioned nothing of it to Jane.

"They're millionaires ten times over. Gosh, what I'd give to marry one of them, even if they're boring and bald!" She was deliberately goading her escort. She laughed with such wicked girlish loudness; one of the under-managers came over and asked them to leave as they were obviously far too young to be in such a place as the Grill. Jane began to protest and caused a scene by saying that she was a Suffragette, but before the under-manager could call reinforcements, Olive took Jane by the arm and whisked her up the stairs from the depths of the Piccadilly Hotel and out into the evening air of the Circus. The young man followed. They gathered by the fountain and perched on its edge

"I better get home or mother will kill me" Olive confessed to Jane. "Ever since Chloe was thrown out the house, it's been the thumb-screws. Where have you been? Who have you seen? What have you been doing?"

"Tell me about it, darling!" Jane was slightly drunk. She'd had a few glasses of champagne that had been bought for her by the young man down from Cambridge for the weekend. "Rupert and I are going on to Claridges, aren't we, darling?"

"Absolutely" declared Rupert Brooke. "Is it the hour? We leave this resting place made fair by one another for a while ...." As he said these words, he looked directly at Olive, but Olive could see that he was more than slightly tipsy and that his romantic nature was spilling over.

"Rupert wants to be a poet," Jane laughed.

"What better occupation for the idle? Do you think there is a far border town" he recited while waving his arms about and walking along the edge of the fountain "somewhere, the desert's edge, last of the lands we know, some gaunt eventual limit of our light, in which I'll find you waiting, and we'll go together, hand in hand again, out there, into the waste we know not, into the night?"

"Come on, Olive, come with us to Claridges, it'll be fun" Jane insisted.

Olive looked at the couple, her sixteen-year-old room-mate at school, and the young undergraduate down from King's College. Her mind flashed to the scowling faces of her mother and father, the years of discipline by the governess, the disappointment that she would cause them by staying out late unchaperoned. Then, in a split second, she abandoned her fears, went with her impulse to be young, and agreed to go with them.

Jane and Rupert both reacted with such enthusiasm, they both fell with a splash into the fountain where they lay floundering and roaring with laugher, revelling in the water.

"Come on, Irish!" Rupert shouted to Olive. She was often referred to as Irish because of her parentage.

Olive hovered on the edge of the fountain uncertain whether to jump.

"Come on, darling" squealed Jane.

There was no going back. She jumped and landed on Rupert who grabbed her round the waist and kissed her. Jane did not seem to mind. There was nothing in the kissing, just sheer joy at being alive and young and happy. They were soaked to the skin but it did not seem to matter. Nothing mattered but that very instant of living for the moment.

As their enthusiasm waned, and the coldness of the water began to make it felt they struggled to the edge of the fountain where two un-amused police constables stood. They were apprehended, taken to Bow Street station and locked up for the night. Separated from Rupert, the two girls sat on their cell beds wrapped in course woollen blankets. They tried to laugh about the situation, but the reality was too harrowing for them. From another cell they could hear the moaning of some woman who shouted abuse and foul language every time one of the constables looked through the grill of her cell. Olive was too scared to sleep and remained awake all night, unaware that the bed she lay on was the same bed that *granny* Clarissa Blum had lain on and confessed her murder of Sissy to uncle Henry.

In the morning Marion and Patrick arrived to collect their wayward daughter. Together they stood with the mother of Jane Cooper (and her latest boyfriend) and witnessed the girls receive from the Chief Inspector a severe caution about their behaviour for almost half-an-hour. When they left they were in tears. The Trainors and Coopers parted without speaking to one another, for each believed the other's daughter to be the corrupting influence, and a direct result of bad parenting. Olive was confined to her room for a week, her meals being sent up to her. There was no Brooky any more to give her whipping and have the matter done with, which had always been the way to deal with family waywardness. The whole episode was blown out of all proportion, and Olive felt wronged, for no-one understood that what they had been doing at the fountain was harmless fun.

She never saw Rupert Brooke again, but Jane Cooper was Jane Cooper, and nothing was going to stop Olive from seeing her again though Olive was taken out of Roedean. Her schooldays were prematurely over and Olive could not forgive her parents for that. She was determined to be out of their house for good, and already in her mind, she had planned her means of doing it.

2

Henry and Eric Fletcher were born identical twins. None could tell them apart except by their natures. It would be easy to describe one as being good-spirited, kind and likeable, and the other as evil, cruel and an utter bastard in business, and to a certain extent these characteristics did manifest themselves in the Fletcher twins, but not in such a black-and-white fashion.

Henry, the first born, was good-spirited but an utter bastard. Eric was kind and likeable, but deep down cruel and evil in social situations Thus, they were both Jekyll and Hydes. When the two Jekylls were on show they were the most dynamic and entertaining couple of men in England.

When their was one Jekyll and one Hyde, they were moody, bickering, self-centred and absolutely the most boring company in the world. When there were two Hydes, then all hell broke loose, and life was a misery for all those who got in their way.

As brothers they were inseparable, and that is why after thirty-eight years of life together, neither of them had married. Henry had bedded a number of girlfriends, but Eric had bedded none. He did not find women attractive, and people had begun to speculate that perhaps he was a homosexual. Deep down Eric did not know what he was, but he was not going to admit it. He concluded that the best way to end the rumour was to marry someone.

In normal circumstances this would not have been a problem for a rich man, but for someone like Eric Fletcher, the thought of kissing a woman was repulsive to him. He detested the way his brother's girlfriends slobbered all over him, and to date, he had been successful in getting rid of Henry's girlfriends one way or another. He was, after all, the spitting image of his brother, and it was not difficult to impersonate him when he chose. As far as Eric was concerned, no woman was ever going to get his brother to the altar.

Henry was no angel, but in some respects, he was not as devious as his brother Eric. He never suspected that Eric had been responsible for the break-up of most of his relationships. As the years had gone past he had grown despondent about finding the right kind of women. In the end, they either seemed to want him for his money or did not like his brother, for like Eric, the thought of marrying someone who would come between him and brother was a non-starter.

 Thus it came as complete surprise to Henry when Eric came into his office one day and announced that he had got engaged. He had to sit down the shock was so great.

"Who's the girl?" he asked, half expecting it to be one of his old girl friends.

"Oh, nobody you know, bruv" he replied in a put-on east-end accent. He was trying to be butch, but he was not very convincing.

"Cut the crap, Eric, who is she?" Henry was annoyed. After years of introducing his brother to all of his girlfriends in the hope of seeking his approval, the least he expected from Eric was the same courtesy. How could he even think of marrying a girl he had not even introduced to him?

"You'll never guess."

Henry made a face. Of course he would never guess if he had never met her. He had never even seen his brother with a girl, and like everyone else had begun to conclude that his brother was queer. Suddenly, he saw Eric in new light. Maybe Eric was just shy? Maybe Eric had been waiting all these years for just the right girl while he had been fooling around and getting nowhere? As far as Henry knew, Eric was still a virgin, for Eric certainly never spoke about these sorts of things.

Henry had suggested double-dating call girls one time, but Eric had turned up his nose in disgust. Henry had explained that it was the latest thing, girls on the end of phone-lines just waiting for it, it was easy, there was nothing to it, you stuck it in, waved it about, and you went home until you felt like calling again, but the whole idea of call girls made Eric sick. Prostitution had come off the streets and could be ordered down the telephone like a bunch of flowers or a new hat.

Every time Henry spoke to a girl on the phone, Eric wondered if she was a call girl or some *bone fide* society lady. There did not seem to be much difference. With a call girl there was a fixed price, with a society lady there was no end to the expense. Eric had been completely enraged when Henry had bought one of his women a brand new car, he thought him a soft touch, and came up with a pretext to take the car back. To this extent, Eric was mean, while Henry was a spendthrift, but this of course was evened out by Eric's huge losses on the racing track. In one year alone, he had lost fifty thousand pounds. Henry knew that his brother was impulsive, and suspected that his engagement was a reckless flutter.

"Who is she then? Spit it out, Eric. Is it some tart you met at Epsom?"

"Nope ...."

"Ascot then?"

"She's got nothing to do with racing. She's too young to be interested in gambling."

"How old is she then" demanded Henry in alarm.

"Sixteen next month."

"She's only fifteen! Christ Almighty!" Henry could not contain his anger. He picked from his desk a steel paperweight in the shape of ship's propeller and slammed it back down on the desk. "Fifteen!! Have you gone horse-brained?? I hope to God you haven't cocked her one, so help me!"

Eric's own anger was rising because his brother was shouting at him. "Don't you tell me what I can do and can't do, you shite. I'm going to marry her and that's that! So get off my back or I'll knock your teeth out."

Henry backed down. He knew his brother had made up his mind. It was no use antagonising him further. Somewhere down the line he would get him to change his mind. For the time being he would play along with him.

"So you love her then?" he asked sitting back down in his chair.

"Sort of" replied Eric "she really is quite wonderful."

"When do I get meet to her?" Henry would soon find out if she were wonderful or not. He did not give much for his brother's knowledge of women, especially as he had never had one before.

"I don't think you should meet her. You might try to steal her from me." Eric was joking; he was very pleased with himself.

Henry glowered. So his brother was serious after all. Years of acting like a queer, he had suddenly found a woman to marry. "Has she agreed to marry you?" he asked.

"Of course she has! Says she can't wait until she's sixteen."

I bet, thought Henry. Probably some illegitimate orphan. "What's her name?"

"Do you remember the Rostov Baby?" Eric spoke with a chuckle "Remember when she nearly fainted in Dad's office and I caught her from falling off her chair? Well, ever since then I've been looking for a girl just like her. See, I fell in love with her moment I saw her. I thought she was so beautiful, and I've never seen another woman as beautiful as her. Don't you agree she was the most beautiful thing you've ever seen?"

Henry could not remember. He had thought the Rostov Baby to be very good looking, but he could not recall much more than that. "Yes, I think she was quite beautiful" he replied to keep his brother happy.

"When I caught her, the smell of her hair was so exquisite. When I asked her if she was all right, and she looked at me with her big dark eyes and said 'Yes, fine, fine ... thank you' in that Irish accent of hers, I melted. Ever since then I have not been able to look at another woman without comparing her to the Rostov Baby."

"Don't you think you've been rather precious holding on to an image like that for twenty odd years? And anyway, when are you going to get to the point? What's the Rostov Baby got to do with it? She's probably a pensioner by now." Henry could be quite cruel when it suited him. "What's the girl's name? Has she got any connections?"

"She's the Rostov Baby's daughter."

Henry's jaw dropped. "Which one" he asked hurriedly. "Not that one that was running around with the King?"

"No. That trollop died a few months ago"

Eric said bitchily. "Her youngest one …
Olive."

Henry screwed up his face and rubbed the
cleft of his chin with his thumb. "You can't
be serious. Dad screwed Elizabeth Shum
out of her fortune. Do you think she'll let
her daughter marry you? You're crazy."

Henry felt a wave of triumph sweep through
him. He did not have to worry about his
brother marrying this young girl any more;
it was totally out of the question.

"We don't need her mother's permission.
We're going to get married in Gretna
Green."

Henry's world collapsed again. Things were
moving too fast. There was something not
right in all this. Why would a fifteen-year-
old girl want to marry his thirty-eight year
old brother? There had to be a motive. As
far as Henry was concerned, it was not
love.

"She's doing it get her mother's money
back?"

"Bollocks! She detests her mother. And
besides, she doesn't even know who I am. I
told her I was just a shipping manager, not
half owner of the company."

"Sure, Eric" Henry replied in the most
sceptical tone. "He falls for a bald-head
shipping manager. She's the daughter of a
countess for god's sake. It's our money
she's after!"

"You're wrong, Henry, I know you're
wrong." Eric was feeling hurt. "She's a
terribly nice girl. Butter would melt in her
mouth. She hates living with her parents.
They're strict Irish Catholics. She wants to

get away from them. You know I don't like girls much, but this one is different. It's time I got married, don't you think? It'll prove to everyone that I'm not a queer, won't it?"

Henry shrugged his shoulders. Maybe the time had come after all. They could not go through their lives without one of them marrying and producing an heir to the business. Besides, what harm could a fifteen year old do to them? They would be more likely to have problems with someone who was nearer their age. A young, innocent girl was perhaps the best option after all.

"Alright, Eric, I won't stand in your way if, first, you introduce her to me, and second, you let me have her checked out by a private detective. Okay?"

"I'm not going to agree to that ...."

"I'm only protecting you, bruv" Henry declared with a deep intake of breath. "I'll have it done with your permission or not. So what do you say? If she checks out, then I'll be your best man. What do you say?" Henry held out his hand.

Eric took his hand reluctantly. "No messing around with her. Promise?"

"I promise." They shook hands. "Leave it to me, Eric. I'll find out for you if she's good enough to be a Fletcher."

Eric smiled cautiously. He remembered all the times he had spoiled his brother's chance of marriage. Now the shoe was on the other foot, and he wondered if he was making a mistake by letting Henry vet his fifteen-year-old fiancé.

3

Olive had told her parents nothing about Eric Fletcher with whom she planned to elope to Scotland the night before her sixteenth birthday on the twenty-second of September. It was already the ninth of the month, and she had been secretly meeting Eric every second day or so for the last four months.

Despite her earlier disinterest in him when she had first met him in the Piccadilly Grill, she had by chance met him again six months later riding a magnificent chestnut bay while she was wheeling Granny Clarissa in Richmond Park. She grew to like him after meeting him again and again as she walked and he rode in Richmond Park, which became too risky in case word of it got back to her parents. Instead, they arranged to meet in the National Portrait Gallery, or the British Museum, for Eric was a great lover of art. During that time they met only through the day, until on the ninth, something out of the ordinary happened.

For some reason, Eric seemed different that day. He met her at Victoria Station and immediately began asking all sorts of questions which he had never asked before. No sooner was she in his motorcar he tried to kiss her. At first Olive struggled to throw him off, but when he reminded her that he was her fiancé, she demurely accepted his advances, and after a little peck or two, she came to enjoy the thrill of his face pressed against hers.

For the first time she imagined that being married to Eric might actually be fun, for instead of taking her to some boring museum or gallery or other monument of national interest, he took her in his motor ar to Brighton. It was the first time that she had been in a sports car, and as it raced by all the other traffic on the road, she felt a thrill of excitement that made her grip on to Eric's arm from the moment they left Canterbury to the first sighting of the White Cliffs and Dover Castle.

He drove immediately to the Grand Hotel, took her by the hand, and inside asked for the key to his suite. Everyone seemed to know him.

"Hello, Mister Henry" said the head-porter.

"Mister Eric" Fletcher corrected the porter with a wink. "Easy mistake to make, old chap."

The porter said nothing, but took a quick glance at Olive and saw that she had no bags. "This way, sir" he said as he led them to the elevator and up to the eighth floor and showed them into a grand apartment that overlooked the entire front. "Mister Henry's suite, Mister Eric, sir."

"Thank you, Dodds. Champagne, please, it's Miss Olive's birthday today" Fletcher tipped him excessively.

"Thank you, sir!" the porter bowed with a smile. He lifted his cap "Miss ... Congratulations" and closed the door behind him.

"It's not my birthday today, Eric" she said in a way that was more of a question than a statement.

"Oh, but it is, my dear" he said kissing her passionately.

Olive did not know what was going on. She felt as though Eric was not the same man she had come to know over the last few months. He was more assertive and seemed to know what he wanted. He lifted her off her feet and threw her on to the bed as if she were a child.

"Eric!" Olive screamed with delight "What's got into you."

He jumped on top of her and began tickling her sides. She giggled and squirmed and tried to fight him off in the playful way she had done with her sisters. She grabbed the pillow and began bashing him over the head with it, but he would not stop tickling her ribs and she was forced to turn on her stomach to escape the gaiety of his fingers. Suddenly she found his hands under her skirt and inside the back slit of her knickers, massaging the cheeks of her bottom. He ripped the knickers to expose her buttocks. Before she could resist, one of his hands went between her legs and as his fingers came up to grab hold of her belly, its thumb entered her and pressed against the upper wall of her vagina. His other hand took her by her long hair and drew her up towards him until he could get his free hand round her to rip the buttons of her bodice and plunge his fingers into the soft flesh of her breasts. She was powerless to resist, he had total master of her. His thumb went deeper and penetrated the entrance of her cervix. She felt something tear as he thrust his thumb up into her womb. She gave out a little scream, and in total ignorance of what he was doing, felt the withdrawal of his thumb, and with a deftness that made her scream again, discovered his penis thrust up inside her. She was in total pain, but it was a kind of pain she had never known before. She started to cry, then stopped when she felt a great heat spread through her body. Eric moaned and came almost immediately to a stop.

At that instant there was a tap on the door. Eric pushed Olive forward on to the bed, extracted his penis, gave her a gentle slap on one of her up-turned cheeks, and buttoned his fly. Olive remained motionless in a state of shock as Eric threw open the door. A look of absolute disbelief spread on the face of the service waiter, who had brought the champagne, as he glanced at Olive half-cocked on the bed with her bum in the air, her skirt about her neck, her bare cheeks protruding from the centre slit of her ripped white knickers.

"It's her birthday" declared Eric loudly. The waiter blushed and looked away as he wheeled in a trolley with a magnum of champagne and a birthday cake compliments of the house. Olive sank into the mattress and buried her head under a pillow. The waiter discretely left the room.

"C'mon, cheerful" said Eric wheeling the trolley over to the bed. Eric lit the candles and sang Happy Birthday. "Get up and blow out the candles, sweetie."

"It's not my birthday!" screamed Olive from

under the pillow. She felt she had to be angry with Eric or he would think that she liked being raped.

"Oh but it is, sweetness and light. Today is your birthday as a woman! Nine, nine, nine. Ninth September, Nineteen Nought Nine ... a day to remember the rest of your life."

Nine nine nine Olive repeated in her mind, and she laughed. She could not believe it herself, but she laughed at Eric's sense of humour despite what he had just done to her. Eric removed the pillow, picked her up, and placed her before the cake.

"Wipe away those tears. Don't be ashamed. You've come of age. Blow out the candles."

She looked at Eric with a sideward glance through her auburn hair. "You are not Eric, are you? You are Henry," she pouted in her prim Roedean voice.

Henry did not reply he smiled. The look she gave him was the same look Henry had seen in his father's office when he was thirteen. Her mother had the same olive eyes. Henry had lied to Eric when he had said that he could not remember much about Marion Shum. He could remember almost everything about her. Yes, she was one of the most beautiful women he had ever seen and he had never forgotten the look on her face when she had jumped up and snatched her coat from the back of her chair and ran out the door. The result of that meeting had long been very beneficial to the Fletchers. Now, he half expected Olive to do the same thing, but he wanted her to stay.

"Go on" he said again "Blow out the

candles."

She bent over and blew out the plethora of candles. Henry uncorked the champagne.

"What is Eric going to say?" asked Olive as she let Henry enter her again some fifteen minutes later. He had his face so close to hers, she noticed for the first time the little broken blood vessels on his cheeks. Eric did not have those.

"Eric doesn't need to know does he?" Henry replied.

"Oh yes he does, my love" Olive replied licking his chin with her prim little tongue "for you are the one that's going to marry me, not him."

She began to nibble his ears, wrapping herself so tightly around him, driving him to thrash between her legs furiously. She whispered in his ear all the things that a man wants to hear from a woman about how masterful he is, how strong, how wonderful a lover he is.

"Where did you learn to say all these things" Henry whispered back as he neared climax.

"At school" she drawled softly.

"Not everything" replied Henry between gasps.

"No, darling, not everything. Oh, sweetness and light" she uttered as Henry began to stiffen. "Come, my love, come into your little princess" she said sweetly as she coaxed him to ejaculate into her.

"Oh, God Almighty" he declared "how can a little virgin bring so much out in me." He grabbed hold of her small boy-like breasts and gave a mighty heave.

"Some things are just in the blood" Olive said as he came into her. It was one of those universal truths that came to individuals while making love. "I guess I just inherited the instinct. Do you think that is possible?"

Henry did not care. He was in heaven. He nodded his head. He did not know where he was or what he was doing any more. Olive by contrast knew exactly what she was doing. By hook or by crook she would marry one of the Fletchers. With two weeks to her sixteenth birthday, she did not really care which one of the twins it was going to be. All she was interested in was getting her hands on their money. As Henry slept, she quite liked the idea having a suite in the Grand Hotel. After all, she knew Brighton like the back of her hand, Roedean was only a few miles away to the east along the cliffs. She took it into her head to ring up her old school.

"Hello, Roedean School for Young Ladies? .... Yes, could you tell Jane Cooper of Rutland that her Great Aunt Ollie is expecting her at six o'clock for tea at the Royal Albion Hotel. You will pass the message on ...? Thank you, kindly. Goodbye."

Olive replaced the receiver, got up, and showered in the bathroom. She found an array of women's clothing in one of the many walk-in wardrobes, all different sizes, presumably there for the use of unprepared visitors. She found a black evening dress that was obviously designed for an older woman, but it fitted well, and she liked the feel of it against her skin. She paraded up and down in front of the wardrobe's full length mirror doors admiring herself, until dissatisfied, she had a desire to try on something else.

Thus, she amused herself, not knowing what to wear, or whether to leave just before six without telling Henry Fletcher where she was going.

4

At times of trouble, Marion Trainor regularly turned to Henry James. She was in a terrible state. Her daughter had run off and she did not know where to find her. More seriously however, Patrick had been found dead in a back bedroom of a boarding room in Glasgow where he had retreated after trying to make money from a wild business scheme. His retreat had brought him to the Gorbals. He knew he could not return to London for he had nothing to take back to Marion except a further item of destitution. There he had lingered for weeks until he died of a heart attack and Marion was sent for to bury him. She knew his views on burial were not hers, India had affected him in strange ways, but she did as he would have wished and had his remains cremated. Some scrawled upon scraps of paper had been found beneath his dead body, and Marion told Henry with wet eyes how she had gone into Glasgow Cathedral after she had seen his body coffined and heard a choirboy sing most beautifully, and she had prayed. She also told him that she had met a young Italian woman living in the same boarding house that Patrick had helped with some immigration difficulty or other. He had endlessly entertained her; they had gone for long walks together, he talked on all sorts of subjects, on politics and love; to her there was nothing that he did not seem to know. When the Italian woman, an honest Catholic unable to hide deceit, admitted that Patrick had died while she was in bed with him, Marion had already suspected as much, and embraced her as a sign of forgiveness.

It had always been Marion's nature to forgive; her convent upbringing had resolutely endowed her with this characteristic. In the cathedral, despite the fact that it was a protestant church, she prayed forgiveness for all of Patrick's sins by the tomb of Saint Mungo. At last, she told Henry, with her family gone, she felt free to devote herself fully to Christ.

"You can't turn your back on life, Elizabeth, you're too young for that. You're only forty-seven." Henry was trying to be kind.

"Do you know what struck me most about Patrick's death?" Marion admitted as Henry shook his head "it was the fact that if he had been found dead in a hedgerow he could not have been more picked clean of possessions. If he had not left at home the cane his father had given him when he married me, I would have nothing of him. His watch was gone; his studs and cufflinks were gone; even his old and battered dressing-case had gone. Even his boots ....." Marion put her heads in her hands.

"I've almost been reduced to poverty, I have little enough left to pay the servants. What a wretched life!"

Henry James tried to comfort Marion, but it was difficult task.

"And Olive. How can I forgive her for this. She doesn't even know her father is dead." She showed Henry a note in which Olive said she never wanted to see her mother and father again. "What have I done wrong, Henry?"

Henry read the note, sat back in his chair, and looked out the study window of Lamb House at the garden he had come to love so much. Throughout his life, his own family had been the source of his greatest pain as well as the greatest joy. He did not know what it was like to lose a husband, but he had lost a father, a mother, two brothers and a sister, and he accepted death, not as a part of life, but as part of living. He was now seventy-one, and though his heart beat vigorously, his head ached.

"Children are usual driven from the home, they rarely go voluntarily" he counselled Marion. "Perhaps you have been too strict. Phyliss and Cecily were at the Patrick's funeral, weren't they? Give it time, Marion. Children are wont to be themselves. You always seem to find the strength to forgive, that's why everyone loves you so much."

"I can't take much more, Henry. I worry myself sick about Olive. Where is she? Who is she with? Eric Fletcher has called at the house looking for her. I'm going to inform the police."

"Don't do that just yet" Henry suggested "I've some youthful admirers at Cambridge I'm going up to see the day after next. " He beamed with embarrassment. "They make me feel like some intellectual Pasha when I visit them." He fluttered his eyes. He had no secrets from Marion, she had known of his homosexual preference since the time he had introduced Stevenson to her in Bournemouth. "Anyway, one of them is that boy Brooke she got arrested with. He's still consorting with that scamp Cooper from time to time. Perhaps we'll find out that way."

"Can I stay here until you leave then come with you, Henry" Marion pleaded. "I can't stand being in London at the moment. Phyliss and Cecily are driving me mad by not letting me do anything for myself. And Bonny's away with the fairies now, she keeps asking when Patrick's coming back. You don't know what an effort it was for me to get out of the house and come and see you on my own."

Henry had never been able to refuse Marion anything. Of all the women he had ever known, with the exception of his sister Alice, she was the most precious. She had none of that brash modern suffragette manner about her that viewed men as nothing better than horse-droppings. She was a real lady, genteel, thoughtful, and soft-spoken. Young men of the day would probably find her stuffy and over-perfumed, but Henry adored her.

"We'll visit Chesterton this afternoon, Wells this evening, and Kipling tomorrow!" he declared, rising to his feet. "It'll be just like old times when you first came across from Ireland!" He was in rapturous mood. "Young heiress to merry widow!" he summed it up. He took her by the hand, stretching out his arm like a ballet dancer, and gave her a twirl. "And if I may say so, bonny lass" he continued in a mock Irish accent "that if I was not a raging queen, I'd marry you this afternoon!"

Marion laughed. Henry was so kind to her, and always had been. She kissed him on the forehead, for in her high-heeled boots, she was a couple of inches taller than him. They hugged one another, and then Henry led her out into the garden to show her the apple trees that never bore any fruit.

5

Olive had not been to Scotland since she was a child. They had gone regularly to Arran to be bitten by the midges and buffeted by the rain. The last time the family had all gone together was the year that Granny Clarissa had got out of Colney Hatch lunatic asylum. They always stayed at the same little cottage at Blackwaterfoot that her parents owned and rented out to holidaymakers, mainly to Glaswegians, during the summer months. In the off-season it was let to the locals at a fraction of the summer rent, but no one was grateful for that, for it was a damp place during the summer months and must have been totally uninhabitable in winter. Yet, there was always some grateful land worker or their likes happy to have a roof over their head, and Olive often imagined some big kilted Scot sitting before the cottage fire cooking wild game or toasting bannocks.

After some days in Brighton, Henry Fletcher did not take Olive to Gretna Green. Instead, he took her by train, boat and car to the Fletcher's estate in Argyll, a holding of thousands of acres between the lands of Ardkinglas and the Clachan of Glendaruel. Nearby was the ancient stronghold of Castle Lachlan which faced, across the waters of Loch Fyne, the hundreds of square miles of Argyll that ran from Inverary to Campbeltown, that belonged to, or had once belonged to Campbell, Duke of Argyll.

At first Olive thought that he had taken her there to hide from any possible gossip, but it soon became apparent that he was totally infatuated with her and could not do enough to make her happy. He could not take is hands off her, and behaved like a schoolboy, much to the embarrassment of the factor and the servants in the house. They spend much of their first three days in the master bedroom having food, books, newspapers; whatever took their fancy, sent up to the room.

It seemed an unlikely relationship, but they talked incessantly about this or that, and when conversation failed them, they made love. On the fourth day, Henry proposed to her. Well, it was a proposal of a sort. He told her to get dressed and meet him down in the large drawing room at the front of the house. Olive had no idea what awaited her, but she had begun to wonder if Henry was just using her for sex.

Dressed in a Harris tweed outfit that Henry had ordered along with a selection of others from Jenners in Edinburgh which had been brought by parcel delivery that morning, Olive descended the twisting baronial tower stairs that led from the upper floor corridor directly to the drawing room below. As she unlatched the oak panelled door, the conversation that she heard as she pushed it ajar, ceased.

Henry did not rush over to kiss her as he had been doing for almost every minute in the last week. Instead, he was seated in an old hand carved chair that looked every inch like some lord-of-the-manor throne. He was wearing a dark-green kilt and had one leg crossed over the other to reveal a small black dirk struck in the top of his knee-length white woolen socks. He sported a white collared-shirt over which he had pulled a v-neck bright red Shetland-wool sweater.

Opposite sat a small man in a dark grey suit. He looked all of sixty, and had a pleasant untroubled face that looked well fed and wrinkle-free. Both men rose.

"This is the Reverend Hugh Conkie, the minister of Gledaruel Parish" Henry said introducing them.

Olive had not noticed it at first, but could now plainly see the little white band that ran under the grey shirt collar of the minister. He gave her hand a little squeeze, and then let his hand linger on hers as he spoke.

"The Laird spoke of your beauty" he said

with the intention of flattery, but it was obvious to Olive that he thought her very young and spoke to her as if she were a child.

"Well, Hugh, man, what do you think? Can you do it next Wednesday?" Henry asked. Olive suddenly became aware of Henry's hint of a Scottish accent. Until then she had always thought of him as English, but now she was not quite so sure."

"Well, I'll have to be asking yourself and the bride-to-be some questions first" he said pensively.

Olive had some difficult in understanding the minister's lilting Western Isle accent. He was not a native of Argyll, but had been sent into the parish twenty years before from the Isle of Lewis. "Now, Olive, will you please be seated by the side of your betrothed." Henry had re-seated himself on a chaise-long and Olive joined him, trying not to touch him as she perched on the other end. "Now, I am to understand that you have not known one another for many years, is this not so? How long exactly."

Olive looked to Henry to answer. "I've known Olive's family twenty five years" Henry stated "long before Olive was born."

"I see." A look of wonderment flickered across Hugh Conkie's face. "And how long then has it been that you have been intended."

"Is all this necessary, Hugh?" interjected Henry.

"Well, marriage is a very big step, is it not? Now, would I not be a negligent man if I did not enquire after such things? These are

God's questions, not for my own curiosity."
He looked severely at them. "Now, please,
how long have you been intended?"

"Four days" replied Olive.

Hugh Conkie's eyes lit up like fireworks. He
took a sharp intake of breath that could
have been heard as far away as Glasgow.
"Four days is it! By jings, the modern world
sets folks in a spin these days. Four days
you say?" He repeated the words with a
solemnity that made four days sound like a
lifetime. "My, my, it must be love you are in
then?" he concluded.

Olive looked to Henry.

"I would say so" he said stiffly "she's a
wonderful girl."

Hugh Conkie's eyes registered nothing. All
the while he had been asking his questions,
he had been noting the answers down on a
piece of paper.

"Now" he continued "Can you tell me how
many years you have both of you."

"Thirty-eight" Henry said nervously, for he
believed that up until then Olive had only
thought him to be about thirty. Indeed,
Olive had believed him to be thirty-two, for
that was the age Eric had confessed to be.
She tried to hide the shock of the discovery
by averting her gaze to the floor. In fact,
almost as soon as she had entered the
room and been introduced to Hugh Conkie,
her head had gone down, and she had
spent much of the time following the cracks
in the floorboards. She now became aware
of him gazing at her.

"Fifteen" Olive said shyly.

"Well" said the minister suddenly sitting

back "that's a fine age to be, and I married my second wife in Stornoway when she was fifteen." Olive looked at him in disbelief. "Och, well now, that was a long time ago, and nowadays the law in Scotland forbids marriage unless the intended are both sixteen or over."

"I'm sixteen next Wednesday" she added quickly.

Hugh Conkie looked happy. "Praise the Lord. And for chust a moment, I was thinking I had wasted my journey up from the village. Now, I know the laird is Church of Scotland as his father was an elder of the Kirk, but whit denomination are you, lass?"

Up until then, Olive had never given it a thought. Religion had never really interested her, though it had been hard to avoid because of her mother. "Roman Catholic" she answered innocently. Hugh Conkie's face went red. "Have I said something wrong?" Olive asked Henry.

"May I have a private word with you, laird?" the minister demanded.

Olive watched as Henry and Hugh Conkie went to the far side of the room and conducted a whispered debate that lasted more than five minutes. The minister remained on the far side of the room while Henry re-approached Olive.

"What's the matter?" she asked.

"He won't marry us. He says he won't have anything to do with Roman Catholics. Says mixed marriages are doomed to spiritual heartbreak. If you were Church of England that would be okay, or Baptist, or non-conformist, but no Roman Catholics." Henry was upset.

"Let me talk to him" said Olive.

"What good will that do? He'll probably start blaspheming the Pope."

"Let me try?"

Henry raised his shoulders and let them drop. "Okay ...." The state of affairs was far from pleasing for him; the last thing he wanted was a repetition of previous affairs that had ended without marriage. It brought back sensations he hoped never to suffer again; going weak at the knees, his stomach turning over, his heart thumping in his throat, a dizzy spinning of sickness, and an incredible impulse to bolt. Was it fair that he should subject Olive to Conkie's pantomime? After all, in Scotland no one needed the Church's sanction for marriage, there were registrar offices, a state of affairs that did not exist in England.

However, he thought Olive was bearing herself well even though her fifteen years seemed to make a silly farce of the situation. Love can bear anything but ridicule, and Henry could see the crude workings of Conkie's mind about the age difference between them. He was experiencing an inexplicable guilt at taking something that did not belong to him; waiting for Conkie's gleeful foot to trample him, the ever absent laird, over a trampled under-foot people.

Henry watched as Olive approached the minister and began to talk quietly to him. Henry strained to hear what was going on, but the drawing room ran almost the length of the whole front of the house and was big enough to accommodate a party of three hundred people. It had been a long time since that number of people had come to the house, not since before the death of his father in '98. Now, it was not used much at all, occasionally to entertain major clients interested in hunting and shooting. His father had willed the whole estate to Henry, for Eric had never liked Scotland much, preferring instead the gentle garden country of the Home Counties.

Suddenly Henry found Olive on his arm. He turned to see the minister a pace or two off.

"Well, now, I think next Wednesday would be a grand for a uniting," uttered Conkie.

"Why the big switch around, Hugh?" asked Henry.

"I'm joining the Kirk" announced Olive. "It would not do for the Laird's wife to be of a different religion as her husband."

"Is it as easy as that?" Henry asked Hugh Conkie.

"Religion is a matter of the mind, Laird. If the mind is won over, then the spirit is won over too" declared the minister. He took out a diary from his coat pocket. "Now, I can fit you in on Monday morning for your baptism. No ...." he corrected himself "it is an important matter, come tomorrow instead at ten o'clock to the kirk." He turned to Henry "I'll discuss the matter of fees with the Factor. Och" he said suddenly remembering something "perhaps I can interest you in helping to restore the old bell. In fact, let me chust have a word with you about that, Henry. Would it be likely that you'll be wanting them rung?" Suddenly he changed his mind again, noticing Olive clinging to him. "But that can wait until tomorrow, we can discuss the arrangements for the ceremony then."

Hugh Conkie put on his stove-pipe hat. Olive nearly laughed for she had never seen one being worn before, the fashion having died out with Abraham Lincoln. They bade him farewell, as he set off in his buggy to the Factor's. Then Henry had some horses saddled up to take Olive around the estate lands to show her, of which the estate was a mere fraction, the wealth she was about to marry into.

*

The marriage of Olive and Henry, against all expectations, proved to be extraordinarily happy. There had been considerable speculation that she had manipulated him, or he had hypnotized her, or that the whole relationship was based on sex, but in truth, despite herself, Olive had fallen in love with Henry Fletcher, and he with her.

After some time, most people came to accept this, including Marion, who had a tearful reconciliation with her daughter at the Fletchers' new home tucked away in that exclusive section of Brighton between North Road and Trafalgar Street. Olive could not be happier, she had everything she wanted, and soon forgot the original reason she had married one of the Fletcher twins, which if we recall, was to recover some of her mother's stolen wealth. Now,

that did not seem to matter, Olive had
access to it all and tried to entice her
mother to move to Brighton to be close by.
Marion would have none of it; her life was
in Tedddington, and she would remain at
the house in Bridgman Road until they
carried her out in a coffin. Olive thought her
mother melodramatic and put down her
stubbornness to old age. As a compromise,
Olive got her mother to agree to have
Henry pay for the entire re-decoration of
her house, and elicited a half-promise that
she would come regularly to Brighton to
stay.

Deep down Marion was not happy, she felt
that Olive had betrayed her, and that it was
a cruel world that had made her lose her
wealth and one of her daughters to the
same family. Phyliss and Cecily were a
comfort, and of course, there was still aged
old Clarissa hanging on for life despite the
onset of senile dementia.

Phyliss was happy for her younger sister.
She had never aspired much to the London
society scene and had settled for marriage
to a young lieutenant in the army. Cecily
had turned out to be the one most like her
mother, affable, well liked, and going
through life being nice to everyone. After
some time in nursing, she had returned to
live with Marion to take care of Clarissa.
Cecily thought Olive too young to have
married, but once she had met Henry
Fletcher, she was amazed how young and
virile he was for his age. She regretted that
she had not met him first.

As for the Fletchers, Eric was furious with

his brother for stealing his bride-to-be. More importantly, he despised Olive for consenting to marry Henry in preference to himself. He could never forgive her for that. Behind his back he felt that people were laughing at him, while to his face, they pitied him. He flatly refused to visit them in their Brighton home, and on some business pretext, he went to America to work out of the company's office in New York.

6

Four, almost five years passed, until on the eve of Olive's twenty-first birthday, two shots from a browning automatic pistol was to change everyone's life for good.

It was the second time that two shots from a Browning had changed Olive's life. The first, as we know, were the Wellesley murders. Murders? This was how the press had reported it, and the coroner's inquiry had, for the same political reasons as the press, given the same judgment. The culprits were never apprehended, and it had passed, as so many unexplained or embarrassing deaths for the government frequently did, as the work of Irish nationalists.

This time round the shots had really been the work of nationalists, Serb Nationalists. It was the age-old conflict for a free Serbia, a greater Serbia that included Bosnia, Herzegovina, Kosova, part of Bulgaria, and Macedonia, the conflict that Grigori had embroiled himself in as a Russian spy, and the backdrop against which he had first met

Olive Vanya in Belgrade. Nothing much had changed except that the Turks had moved out and the Austro-Hungarians had moved in and annexed Serbian Bosnia for themselves, and the Serbs, despite having their own independent state, were being thwarted on all sides to unify their greater Serbia.

Now, as to most lay people, some lost cause in the Balkans was no concern of theirs, and to this extent, the larger nations continued to crush the rights of the smaller ones as they had always done. They could not see that the age of European Empires was coming to an end. The waves of nationalism that had been sweeping Europe and come to nothing since 1848, finally erupted, and it was the Serbians who had enough of being pushed around. In hindsight, history apportions blame, but who can say that the Great War, if it had not begun in Serbia, could have begun in Latvia, Poland or Ireland, three smaller nations swallowed up in the larger empires of the Russians, Germans, and English.

The two shots from a Browning pistol fired by a Bosnian Serb, which killed Emperor Franz Josef's nephew and his wife in Sarajevo, was an act on par with David killing Goliath. The greatest Philistine of them all, Franz Josef, reacted by invading Serbia. Those men, who believe that man's difficulties should always be solved by talking rather than fighting, are the same men who rob you while you are sleeping. When a nation is believed to be getting away with robbery, it is action not words that brings retribution, and on the eve of Olive's twenty-first birthday, the whole of Europe was ready to take up arms against the robbery of Serbia by Austria. Men were eager for a fight, to settle old scores that had not been properly addressed since the days of Napoleon. No-one was truly interested in the rights of small nations, least of all Serbia, which most people knew nothing of, their eyes were fixed on larger foes. The punch-up between Austria and Serbia was an excuse to have an all-out bar-room fight in which everyone had already picked their sides. It was this short-sighted drunken macho-man attitude that ultimately destroyed Europe's dominance of the world for the rest of the century, but which more significantly, was to destroy the happiness of three generations in across the globe for the next thirty years.

*

Henry was busy in conversation with the woman who sat on his right. She was the wife of the U.S. Ambassador to London. "It can't go on like this," declared Henry "Something's got to be done about the U-Boats. We're on the ropes already. If we lose any more ships we'll go down like the Lusitania."

"My, that was awful wasn't it?" she declared. "I knew Albert Vanderbilt. What a tragedy. Women with babies in their arms too."

Henry had struck the right note. The British needed the Americans into the War if they were going to starve the Germans into submission. The blockade of the German ports was working beautifully, but at what cost?

"We're losing as many as twenty ships a day to German U-boat torpedoes. And it's not all happening way out in the Atlantic, it's happening within sight of Brighton, Falmouth, Yarmouth, and they don't care whether the ships are British or American."

Olive had prepared the party for twenty-five in their house in Belgrave Square which Henry had bought after they were married. She had planned it well in advance so she could devote most of her time to entertaining her guests. The party was the better for it. She thought it sad that so many parties she went to, she hardly ever saw the hostess - she was always in the kitchen supervising the cook. Whenever she saw a flustered hostess, she always felt guilty and uncomfortable.

She had planned her party several weeks in advance. She had given Mrs. Dudgeon, her cook, two weeks notice - it was only fair to her. She had to do the shopping, order all the food etc. Olive never got involved in that. She stayed away from kitchens. As well as supervising the food, drinks and the table, Olive had given herself a good forty-five minutes of breathing space before the guests arrived, to have a look around and check that she had not forgotten something. In fact, she was expecting anything to happen - with the War going on - guests might ring to say they would be late, in which case she would have time to rearrange the table. Before her breathing space, she allowed herself ample time to dress. Every hostess needed time to look her best. If she felt she looked her best she felt more relaxed and the guests would sense that. Naturally, dress was important; after all, she hoped to be the most attractive woman there.

Nearly every man in the room was in some sort of uniform or other, except the Ambassador, old Henry James, and her husband. However, Henry Fletcher wore a khaki armband bearing the Crown which showed his willingness to serve in the Forces, but already in his mid-forties, and well-placed in the hierarchy of the establishment, with a million Britons already entrenched in the Western Front, it was merely for show. Meanwhile, Olive was at the other end of the table, held in conversation by the U.S. Ambassador.

Olive had gradually become more experienced at entertaining. She found herself sticking to more and more rules. She invited people for eight o'clock then allowed forty-five minutes for drinks before she sat her guests down to dinner. This gave everyone time for two drinks, glasses of whatever they fancied. She did not proscribe to the idea of drinking solidly for hours as they did in some countries before sitting down to eat at ten or after. Most people would have drunk so much they would no longer be interested in eating at all; it was not fair to poor Mrs. Dudgeon.

"No plans for children then, Mrs. Fletcher" the Ambassador enquired in that direct American way that was well intentioned, and not meant as a means of prying into Olive's sexual life which was so often the case. With all these dashing young men in uniforms, many who never returned from the fighting, being married to an older man gave Olive security, but left her open to the advances of young heroes who had contempt for her husband. She felt that such things never happened before the War, but then again, she had hardly gone anywhere without being on Henry's arm. Now, she saw a lot less of him and had got involved more and more with people her own age.

Jane Cooper, now Mrs. Warneford-Cooper had settled in Belgrave and had a string of young men chasing after her. She had arrived late with her party of three, and they had only got one drink instead of two. If they had arrived any later, her guests would have gone into dinner and that would have been just too bad, Jane and her friends would not have got dinner. Brooky had been very strict with Olive, and the importance of punctuality had been instilled in her when she was very young. If she had been one minute late for lunch, she had got a whipping, so as a habit, she found it impossible to be late. Nine times out of ten, when she was a guest, she was the first to arrive.

Jane had been seeing Rupert Brooke again and it looked as though their old romance had been rekindled. But Rupert had taken a commission in the Royal Navy Division and sailed for the Dardanelle's, dying on route from blood poisoning after being bitten by a mosquito. His last poem for Jane had read: "If I should die think only this of me that here's some corner of a foreign field that is forever England." They had buried him on the island of Skyros, and Jane had been heartbroken at his loss. A month later, in an attempt to forget Rupert, Jane married Reggie, a flight lieutenant in the Royal Flying Corps. He had been awarded a Victoria Cross for bringing down a German Zeppelin with bombs. Two months later he was shot down in Belgium and killed. Jane was devastated for a second time, though not quite as badly as the time before and Olive did all she could to console her friend, but the loss of two men she loved dearly within three months of one another, was a severe blow.

Olive had music playing in the background. She'd instructed one of the servants to set up the gramophone in the next room. She felt that having it in the same room, the music would dominate instead of the conversation. At that moment it was playing *Pack Up Your Troubles In Your Old Kit Bag*.

"How can any woman bring children into the world in times like these" Olive said quietly to the Ambassador. She had to make sure that the conversation kept flowing and that none were left out. It was thought by some that politics or religion should never be talked about at dinner parties and that talk should be steered away from sticky subjects, but Olive thought that was nonsense. People should talk about what they wished, as long as they did not insult each other.

"Surely you have thought it thru?" The Ambassador pursued his line of inquiry like a legal man, for he had been a judge before President Wilson's election.

Olive had thought it through. She had decided that she was in no hurry to have children. She had seen what it had done to her mother, a beautiful woman who had been aged prematurely by the worries of family. Henry did not seem to be too concerned either, and besides, after six and a half years of marriage, they were enjoying the freedom that rich, childless couples, seem to enjoy at the expense of everybody else's misery.

She noticed that a young army officer in the middle of the table had an empty glass. It was difficult to keep an eye on everyone. She signalled one of the hired staff for the night to fill his glass

"Do you really hate the Germans so much!"? The young man rose bringing the heel of his empty glass down on the table. It was too late, and the hired help backed off a little as all conversation stopped.

Olive had been watching to make sure that no one was being cornered by a bore and could not get away. Normally she had to extricate such people because they were too stupid to get up and fetch themselves a drink, but nobody had ever jumped up at one of her dinners like that before.

Everyone turned to stare at the young man who had been sitting at the centre of the long dining table a little below the salt. He had been seated between Jane Cooper-

Warneford and Rebecca Fairfield, a young woman from Richmond who wrote under the name of West. She was Olive's age and had formed a relationship with H.G.Wells to extent that, when H.G. had been invited to the party, Olive had been obliged to invite her too. Mister Wells sat up the table on Henry's left, while Henry James, for whom the party had been thrown to celebrate his taking out of British citizenship, sat on Olive's right opposite the American ambassador with Marion on the Ambassador's left. As yet, Olive had not quite mastered the art of placing guests to the best advantage, and had decided that in future, she would place her mother at the other end of the table so she could not tell tales about her. Most of the other guests who were seated at the middle sections of the table were literary types of one sort or another, including Miss Bosanquet, Henry James's secretary, but none of them sparkled for Olive the way that Rupert had with his physical beauty and brilliant talent.

Nevertheless, they were nothing now compared with this young man. Earlier, Olive's attention had been drawn to the young officer. The others called him Mad Jack. He had been recently wounded at the Front and was almost fully recovered. He had enlisted at the very beginning of the War and had somewhat animated actions, but Olive saw a wild sensuality in him that could not be contained by his dull khaki uniform. Like Rupert, the young man's passion was for poetry and he had known

Rupert at Cambridge. He had been one of the latecomers in Jane's party of friends.

"Be quiet and sit down Siegfried!" Jane said angrily, tugging at his tunic.

"I will not!" At first his anger seemed to be addressed to someone across the table from him, but too incensed to direct his ire at one person alone, he took in the whole table, and fixed his attention on Olive at it's head. "Mrs. Fletcher!" he addressed her "I have been accused by one of your guests as being unpatriotic because I don't hate the Boche! How could I hate the Bosch when I'm part German myself? Do you know that the first Christmas on the battlefield we exchanged gifts of cigarettes and beer with the enemy? The enemy? Do you know that one simple soldier boy put a bullet through his own brain rather than fight the enemy. What a joke! The enemy is our own Generals. Along they come. "Good morning!, good morning!" they say as we're on our way to the line. And do you think we smile back at the swine and his incompetent staff? Some conscript Harry will say to some conscript Jack "He's a cheery old card" as they grunt up to the Front with their rifles and packs. What for? To be done in by the General's order to attack! O Jesus! While German mothers are knitting socks to send to their boys at the Front, we're sent to run and trample their terrible corpses deeper into the mud. Oh you women! You love us when we are heroes, home on leave, wounded in a mentionable place. You worship decorations and you want to hear tales or dirt and danger! Well here it is! Bombs! Guns! Shovels! Battle-gear! Massed at dawn, men jostling to climb to their deaths, the order going out ... Over the top! Half dead from the barrage before you leave the trenches to face the lines of grey, their muttering faces, their furtive eyes, toppling towards them, the wire, then finding yourself floundering in the mud, clutching at the wire, snagged, tangled, toiling in anger in your own blood. All around you your men falling like bells, hanging on the wire for hours, the unbroken wire, until there is nothing left but the chance of death, and you sink your face into the mud, until the retreat comes, and it's then that you run and trample the terrible corpses of your own men, blind with blood, deeper into the mud. Then, without fully believing that you are back in your own trench, you count the muddy faces of the dead on the ground and in your head, and wait for the following dawn."

No one moved at the table. There was not a sound, not even a bar of *Pack Up Your Troubles* from the gramophone next door. There was such a silence that Olive swore, years after the war had finished, that she could hear, and feel, the dull rumble of the Flanders guns far across the Channel. She knew there should be no pauses or gaps in the conversation, if she had invited the right people, but this was not expected behaviour. Normally she had a few regulars like Jane she could call on to keep the conversation flowing smoothly, but Jane sat dumb-stuck like a dead-eyed cow. It had always been Olive's policy never to invite an extra woman to dinner, for no woman wanted to sit next to another woman, so to make up the twenty five, she had asked Jane to invite an extra man. For the first time in her dinner-giving career as a society hostess, the extra man had become a bigger headache than two women sitting together.

Siegfried sat down, and as he did so, Olive began to clap. What else could she do? She had to get the party going again, and it seemed, now that he was finished, that Siegfried's speech had been rather splendid, and that he had outshone everyone. Some of the other service men at the table began to clap as well, until everyone picked up the rhythm. Who made the offensive remark, no one was certain, but Olive thought it was Siegfried's young friend Owen. It was an extraordinary action. The ladies joined in too, and Siegfried, who moments earlier had appeared to be made insane by his experiences in the trenches, had stolen the evening. Well, almost everyone though he had. It was obvious from husband Henry's expression that he did not approve of Olive's young army friends at all.

Henry James, who had been quiet since his arrival, had thought it would be the usual English party where the dinner would be dull and the men would sit about drinking port after dinner while the women retired to the drawing room. Now there was buzz about the party that was not there before. "That boy" Henry James turned to Olive and the Ambassador "is what we writers would call an anti-hero." He grinned. "It's a sign of the times. The young have had enough of death. It's not a thing that old people have a monopoly on any more. It's a slaughterhouse over there. Haig sends them in like cattle. But what can we do? Write poetry about it? Nope, nobody writes pro-war stuff like the Charge of the Light Brigade any more. Henry Ford has rolled the horse into history. Wright has given armies wings. Europeans using American innovations, without American know-how."

"Do you think you will come to help us, Mister Ambassador" Marion asked. Normally she was not interested in political matters, but like everyone else, she had woken up to the fact the world had changed for good. The young soldier had demonstrated that. The quiet ordered life of the Victorian classed society had been rolled into history too, and Marion felt vulnerable and defenceless in the face of disorder.

"That is a matter for Congress, Lady Elizabeth." American neutrality was an unattractive face he constantly had to present to the British. He hoped that the Germans would act so aggressively against American shipping that America would have no choice but to join the Allies. Wilson's pleas for neutrality now struck him in London as irresponsible, self-serving cowardice. He felt he was being deprived of the moral America of which he had once been so proud.

"You'll come" Henry interjected firmly. "You'll come like I did when you realise that most Americans are concerned about the old motherland, whether it's England, or Germany, or Italy. You'll see how things go then join the winning side. Whatever side you fight on, you'll be accepted, for by that time everyone will be so tired of war, you'll be seen as the ones who ended it. Everyone will love you for that. America! The land that ends wars never starts them! It's the way of all conflict. The nation that starts the war is viewed as the cause of everyone's sorrow. In this case, it is Austria and Germany, so it is inevitable that America will come in on the side of England and France, but only if Austria and Germany don't start winning. Am I right, Ambassador? After all, I was an American once."

The Ambassador laughed, but Olive could see from his reaction that there was some accuracy in Henry's observation.

"My goodness, everyone has finished dinner" Olive noted. It was time to withdraw before there were any more scenes. "Ambassador, ladies, officers, and gentlemen, please take a partner if you can, and follow my husband, if you will. We have a surprise in store for Henry."

At the time it seemed a wonderful idea, but as she caught the eye of Mad Jack, Olive thought she might have made an error of judgement by arranging a firework display at the rear of the house. But her fears were soon put to rest after the display; Siegfried approached Olive to thank her for the evening.

"You did not mind the fireworks?" she

asked.

"Not at all" he replied sincerely. "At the Front we have no control over the fireworks. Here, it was very ordered and civilized, and I thank you for that. I hope I did not upset your other guests with my outburst. I was upset because I am returning to the France in a few days. I recovered some weeks ago, and I was ordered to return to the Front, but I told them I wouldn't go. Instead of court-marshaling me, they sent me to a sanatorium. In the sanatorium, with the war-mad, the shell-shocked and the half-dead, I realised I was alive despite all I had been through. I began to think of my men, the ones I'd left in the trenches to get on with this stinking rotten war. One or two of them have been with me since '14, not many, but enough to make me care about what happens to them. That's why I have to go back, no other reason."

He looked so lost. She placed the palm of her hand on the back of his hand and pulled the cigarette he was smoking away from his lips, took it from his hand and put it to her own lips. She inhaled lightly then offered the cigarette back to him. For the first time, she saw him smile, a wonderful boyish smile. A twinkle came to his eye.

"Thanks" he said "it means a lot to share a ciggy with one of Rup's girls."

The party was breaking up. Olive felt she had done her thing towards the War, and old friend of the family Henry James. He looked unsteady on his feet, suffering as his doctor said, an aggravated condition of the heart. Olive had arranged a car for Henry, her mother, and Miss Bosanquet back across London, for Henry, no longer well enough to live in his big house in Rye, had moved to an apartment in Chelsea. At the time, as she said her farewells, Olive did not know that it would be the last time she saw dear old uncle Henry, who had known her Russian grandmother.

The dinner had been a success. The sign of a bad dinner party was when the guests could not wait to leave, but that had not been the case. The party had reached its conclusion, and fortunately the guests sensed it too. The Ambassador and his wife were amongst the last to leave.

Later, after everyone had gone, Olive discovered that Henry, her husband, had been trying to conclude a deal with the Ambassador concerning the carrying of American wheat on Fletcher ships. Normally, such business would have been the main reason for the dinner, but this time it left her feeling sick, for Henry was trying to profit from the war, while all the best young men of her own generation were being wiped out or maimed, fighting for something that seemed no longer to have any logic or reason to it. It was pointless to ask if he was happy despite his millions, for his millions made him happy and he was never alone. She thought Henry too pre-occupied with business to spend much time with her, although given the choice, she'd rather have a workaholic husband than an alcoholic one. But surely, there had to be more to life than money?

Olive went to bed very unhappy. Henry asked her what was wrong, but she shrugged her shoulders and said it was nothing. As she lay in the bed with Henry on top of her, she could not erase from her mind the face of the tormented young man Siegfried, and the things he had spoken about. She thought about him; she thought about Reggie; and she thought about Rupert - all beautiful young men, all of them lost to the War, while she lay on her back between silk sheets with a man old enough to be her father. It all seemed such a waste, such a terrible pointless waste; the non-returning army that was youth.

*

It is a fact that the events of the Great War were beyond comprehension by anyone. It was in every respect, a world war. Australasians, Asians, Africans, Europeans, and North Americans, fighting around the globe. Some of the worst of it was in the trenches of the Western Front in Flanders. The launching of an offensive, preceded by a bombardment of three thousand guns, coupled with heavy rain, had wrecked the network of dykes and streams upon which the Flanders drainage system worked. The fields around Passchendaele and Ypres had been turned into a quagmire where men were sucked to their death if they slipped from the duckboards.

All of this was no longer the worry of Franz Josef, the man who had brought the world to war. He was dead, and there were few outside of Austria mourned his passing. The grand days of the Hofburg were now history; the heady days of Vienna as Europe's cultural capital were long gone. The Austrian-Hungarian Empire was about to be totally dismantled. The days of the Emperors were over. In Russia, Csar Nicholas II and his family had been taken to a small town in Western Siberia while Kerensky fought it out with the Bolsheviks. In time, he too would be dead, but not before Russia lost Finland, the Baltic States, Poland and Bessarabia. In Turkey, the Ottoman Empire had already been reduced to one quarter of its former size. Germany, meanwhile, had lost all its overseas colonies, and would at the end of the war, rid itself of Emperor Wilheim. The British, of all the Empires, remained intact, stoically refusing to give up its Emperor and move with the times, but at the cost of losing three-quarters of its shipping to U-boats.

The Fletchers had not been slow to capitalise upon it. At the beginning of the war they had built a dry dock for the repair of damaged shipping, and had been quite successful in tendering for navy contracts. Olive had been presented to Queen Mary when she had relaunched HMS Broke, which had been badly damaged ramming a German destroyer in action alongside HMS Swift. Queen Mary told Olive that she remembered her sister Chloe quite well when she had often been a guest of her mother-in-law Queen Alexandria. She recalled the circumstances of Chloe's death. Olive had often worried about diabetes. "Do you have children, dear?" asked the

Queen.

Olive had always been concerned that perhaps if she had children, one of them would develop the ailment. "Now yet, your highness ... perhaps after the War."

The Queen nodded as if she understood. "It's a terrible business, but we must keep our chins up." She stepped forward to the cheers of the crowd of workers and their families who had been invited to witness the relaunching. The Queen took the champagne bottle on the rope, and with a well a practised action, smashed the bottle on to the hull of the destroyer. It slipped out of the blocks amidst a rattling of chains and entered the waters of the Thames.

The Queen had other duties to perform that afternoon, so she had no time for further conversation with Olive. She hastily accepted the thank you's of Henry and the company representatives and an envelope containing her fee. It was not termed as such, referred to instead as a small gift, which Olive discovered later, was one thousand pounds.

Everything had gone very smoothly thought Henry. There had been no gaffs by the staff, and everybody on the slips had done their jobs well. Even Olive had pleased him, for she looked radiant when she had been presented to the Queen. The crowd had done their job too by waving little Union flags and shouting out terms of endearment. Even the weather had been magnificent, for it was a glorious sun filled afternoon with not a cloud in the sky.

As the Queen was escorted to her waiting

automobile, Olive followed close behind her small entourage of bodyguards and ladies-in-waiting. Suddenly from out of the crowd lunged a young man shouting "Down with the king! God Save Ireland!" He had a revolver in his hand. Immediately he was seized upon by a number of men and brought to the ground. The Queen carried on as if nothing had happened, but Olive, less certain, cast glances in the direction of where the young man had been standing. She looked away, and then looked again, for she could not believe her eyes. There, in the crowd was a man about Henry's age that she recognised. At first she could not put a name to him, then it all flooded back to her. It was Shaun Rigby! The man she had helped to escape from the police in Killarney!

There was no doubt that he was the accomplice of the young man with the revolver. She had read that nationalist assassins rarely worked alone. He had to be part of the plot to kill the Queen.

He stood staring back at her, while around him people were milling to get a glimpse of the young man. From the look in Shaun's eye he had been thrown in two minds. Did he have a bomb that he was about to throw at the Queen's party?

Olive became convinced that indeed he had. Why did he not throw it? Why did he wait so long for the Queen got into her open-topped automobile? The only answer she could come up with was that her presence had momentarily clouded his judgement. It was obvious he remembered her, it was all across his face, and she could he was reliving in his mind the journey to Tralee they made together by horse some fourteen years before.

So why did he continue to hesitate and not throw his bomb? And suddenly it was too late. Someone pointed to him as the companion of the young man who had just been disarmed, and immediately he was seized by plain-clothed and uniformed police and dragged with the young man unceremoniously into a waiting Black Maria. The Queen's plate-glass automobile departed, and the crowd waved and cheered at her bravery, as she returned their waves without a hint of fear.

Olive was left stunned. This time she could not help Shaun Rigby. The cause of Ireland was no longer her cause too. She had to believe in law and order and the hierarchy of things, for despite her Irish parentage, she felt herself to be English. The Irish could not go around taking over post offices and murdering and maiming people just because they wanted to have their own government. What, after all, was wrong with being British?

Without knowing it, the fears that her grandfather had harboured about his granddaughter had been justified. Olive had become more English than the English themselves. Like Diarmid Wellesley she had forgotten her own roots - Ireland was just another part of the Empire to her. In her circle, preserving the Empire was the be all and end all. And of course, there could be no Empire without preserving the Emperor and the Empress. Shaun Rigby had been wrong in trying to kill the Queen, and Olive wrote to her grandmother Vivian to tell her so, but Olive was not prepared for the reply that she got.

Ireland had moved a long way forward since she was ten. There was civil war looming between those that wanted an independent republic, and those who wanted to remain British. The Trainor family found themselves straddling the wide divide. Vivian and Patrick Trainor were as committed as always to a free Ireland. They were now almost in their eighties, and Partick had, withstanding the prejudices of religion, become a K.C., a position he used to defend nationalists accused of murder and treason. Even in the courts, Patrick's work was one that pitted him against the full force of foreign occupation. In most nationalist cases, there was only a semblance of a fair trial. Most Nationalists were shot without trial at all, most notably Padraic Pearse and James Connelly.

When Olive got her grandmother's letter she was appalled to find out what was really happening in Ireland. Surely the British could not be so cruel? In the end, she burnt the letter on the drawing room fire wanting to believe it to be a tissue of lies. The British were not barbaric like the Russians or the Germans. English justice was the fairest in the world and respected everywhere. If the army shot people then it was because they were terrorists and murderers, and as far as Olive was concerned, that was the end of it.

*

Eric had long forgiven his brother for stealing his bride-to-be, but he could never forgive Olive. He had returned from America sometime before the war and slotted into his old ways as if he had never been away. He returned to his old job as a company director, for he retained a forty percent shareholding in the company. What he did within the company structure was somewhat baffling, for it seemed to outsiders that Henry carried most of the responsibility and made most of the company's important decisions.

America had changed Eric. He had returned with a companion called Robert who was considerably younger and very effeminate. Eric doted on him the way Henry had once doted on Olive, and it soon became apparent that they were lovers. Most of the young men in England had volunteered or been conscripted for the War, but as an American, Robert was exempted from any form of service. However, he was not without friends, for he was a popular young man with his fellow ex-patriots, many of whom he knew from his days at Harvard.

Eric was very possessive of Robert in much the same way that Henry had been possessive of Olive. They would have terrible rows when Robert came home late to their shared London apartment. Eric was terrified of losing Robert, and it was their fifteen-year age difference that caused much of the tension in their relationship.

Eric continued to gamble as he had always

done. He had bought some racing horses, which he ran in the flat season. None did particularly well except for Conqueror, a thoroughbred he had bought for Robert. Having picked up Eric's gambling habits, Robert had lost Conqueror in a card game, which had infuriated Eric. For a while he cut him off entirely, forcing Robert to go out and find work to support himself. Dutifully, Robert toured London to put his Harvard degree in classics to use, but it was wartime, he was young, and the only work that was offered to him was as a miner in a Kent colliery. When Eric heard that his delicate lover was considering work down a coal mine, he forbade him to do it and restored his allowance.

Eric was not so tender in his relationship with Olive. They met infrequently, but when they did, Olive was never left wondering about his feelings towards her. He embarrassed her whenever he could.

"Oh, look" he said to some friends while lunching at Simpsons in London "Here comes that tart my brother married." He said it so loudly that the people at the adjoining tables strained their necks to see who he was referring to.

Olive had been shopping with Jane Warneford-Cooper. It was Jane who caught sight of Eric first. She could tell it was Eric from his flamboyant, effeminate clothes which he had bought in America.

"Don't look now, darling" she said to Olive as they sat down at their table "but there's that beastly brother-in-law of yours."

Olive looked up. She was not feeling very

well; she had been having terrible period pains and had not slept a wink the previous two nights. She was very pale and had put on more make-up than usual to give her face some colour. In keeping with the fashion she had a low neckline that exposed a considerable amount of her bust, and a high hemline, which displayed a lot of ankle.

"See, look at the whore" Eric continued to shout, "She's little better than a down-market Mata Hari!"

Several people drew in their breaths, including Robert who quite liked Olive. To compare her to Mata Hari, the exotic Dutch dancer who allegedly passed the secrets of her military lovers on to German intelligence officers was completely unfair. Eric had no proof that Olive had lovers, and Robert knew that he was making it up as revenge for the fool she had made him look years before.

Eric got up from the table and went over to Olive and Jane who were on the opposite side of the dining room.

"Brace yourself, darling" Jane whispered under the brim of her hat.

"Good afternoon, ladies" Eric said innocently enough "My, don't we look just like a pair of dykes sitting together holding hands."

"I beg your pardon?" Jane stammered with a bat of her eyelids as if she had not quite heard him right.

"Wait to I tell our Henry about this" he continued ignoring Jane. "How long have you two been having an affair?"

"You've got a filthy mind!" Jane exclaimed "Waiter! Waiter!" she called excitedly.

"I bet you get down and lick each other like dogs."

"Fetch the manager!!" screamed Jane at the waiter.

Eric turned to face the entire restaurant had stopped to stare. "Look at them! Lesbians! Do you want to eat in the same room as a pair of women who fondle each other."

By the time the manager came to the table, the damage had been done. Olive, already weak from menstruation, fainted in her chair. As the restaurant staff tried to revive her, Eric returned to his table.

"What'd you have to do that for, Eric?" Robert said rising to his feet and rushing over to Olive and Jane's table.

"The bitch deserved it" Eric stated to his other friends who did not know what to think.

Jane Warneford-Cooper had arrived unnoticed behind Eric. Without warning, she started to batter him over the head with her umbrella, knocking him from his chair. As he lay on the floor she picked up his chair and threw it on top of him, then grabbing the tablecloth, pulled the entire contents of the lunch-table down on to him. He let out a squeal of pain as a pot of hot tea scaled his face. He lay there writhing.

"My husband won a V.C.!" she angrily informed his friends, their lunch now on the floor. Jane returned to Olive.

"I must ask you to leave, madam," the manager was saying unequivocally to Olive who had revived. Olive did not protest.

Jane was livid.

"Leave?" she declared defiantly. "You should have that man arrested. You will be hearing from my solicitors."

"Let me help" Robert requested as Jane supported Olive towards the door.

"No thank you, sir" Jane said indignantly.

"Let him help us, Jane" Olive interrupted. "Let him carry our bags to the street. I know him. He's a kind man."

"Robert!" shouted Eric, half-blinded by the scalding tea. "Robert! Come back! Don't leave me!"

Robert's puppy-dog face was torn between doing the right thing, and love. He looked at Olive and Jane. This was his chance to break from Eric for good. He was such a tyrant. Perhaps Olive had seen that in Eric and married Henry instead? Maybe Olive and Jane were lesbians after all? He did not know. How could he go back to Eric after what he had done? He had embarrassed everyone, and humiliated himself in the process. Yet, there was something in his call that told him that he needed him. The two women only needed him as far as the street to carry their bags; after that, he would be alone, a young American in London with coal-mining as his only prospect of work. No, that was a terrifying scenario. Better the devil you know than the one you don't know.

Robert thrust the bags into the hands of one of the waiters and tipped him a shilling.

"Sorry, ladies, but he really does need me."

Jane ignored him, but Olive smiled a little thank you for the concern he had already shown. The waiter with the bags led the ladies out.

Robert returned to the restaurant. Eric was sitting alone, one of his eyes covered with a tea towel. The rest of the party had cut short their lunch and had left. Robert pulled up a chair.

"Why did you do that, Eric? It achieved nothing."

"You don't understand," he said in a hard voice.

"Well, tell me then? Why do you hate her so much?"

"I don't hate her!" he snapped.

"Don't tell me you still love her?" It suddenly dawned on Robert that it might be possible.

"Yes" he said, "she's the only woman I've ever had the slightest love for."

"Oh, Eric" said Robert crossing his arms. For the first time he felt jealousy in his relationship with Eric. "I thought you loved me?"

Eric squinted out from his scalded eye. Robert had never asked him that before. He put his hand on his. "Well, now we know who the bitch is in our relationship, don't we" he said dryly. "Lets get out of this place."

They left, and no one challenged them about the bill. Eric took Robert back to their apartment, where after some soul searching, they made love in the bath.

*

Henry had heard rumours that Olive was being unfaithful to him, but he refused to believe them. The War was over and everyone was rejoicing singing the hit songs *Till We Meet Again* and *After You've Gone*. At the beginning of the War everybody had been singing *It's A Long Way To Tipperary*, but the journey was over, and the coming together in national unity was replaced by a feeling of everyone going their separate ways.

For the last two years of the War, Henry had felt that Olive was drifting away from him. He rarely saw her during the week. If he were at their house in Belgrave Square, she would be at the house in Brighton. If he were at Brighton, she would be at the apartment they rented at the Grosvenor House Hotel in Park Lane. If he were at the Grosvenor, she would be down at the Knightsbridge stables for most of the day. He always seemed to be chasing after her, trying to keep up with her. Her energy far exceeded his own, and often he wished he had married someone his own age that would be happy to spend time talking about the past, rather than worrying constantly about the future.

He had missed the start of the shooting season in Scotland that summer because he had to oversee a consignment of supplies to aid the White Russians against the Bolsheviks. It was one of the links the company still had from the days when Grigori was their go-between. More than anything, Henry loved going to Scotland, and somehow he felt cheated out of his usual annual holiday. It had never entered his head to vacation somewhere more exotic, somewhere that his wife may have found something better to do than entertain the local wives. He never once thought that the drizzly wet weather of August and September which had so suited Queen Victoria, might be viewed by someone of a different age as dismal, dreary, and utterly depressing.

When, by chance, Henry came upon a book left lying near the beside in Belgrave Square called *Married Love*, and he began to wonder if his marriage was on the rocks. Sex was not a subject he talked about to Olive, but more out of indignation than curiosity, he opened the book and read about the sexual responsibilities of marriage. It implied that sex was important beyond the procreation of children and called for contraceptive advice to be made more available.

Henry laughed. Sex in his marriage with Olive had been sex, and nothing else. There had never been any talk of children, Henry had expected it just to happen, but it had not. He now began to wonder why. For some years he had thought that there was perhaps something wrong with his sperm. Worried about sterility, he had gone to a Harley Street specialist who concluded their was nothing wrong with him. Instead, he convinced himself that Olive was infertile, and as that were the case, he had decided to divorce her and marry again so that he could have an heir to his millions. He had already wasted almost ten years. He was approaching fifty and would be dead before his son would be mature enough to run the business. He had made up his mind to confront Olive about his feelings, but time and time again, his strength failed him. The desire to have a child was tearing him up. He had everything else he wanted, and were he not tied to Olive, there would be nothing to prevent him from having what he wanted.

Then, after reading Dr. Stopes *Married Love*, a new notion struck him. What if Olive had been using some form of contraception all these years? It was possible; there were ways, so Dr. Stopes said. What if all this time she had not wanted to have a baby? He had never heard her talk about children at all, not once, and that not strange for a woman who was twenty-five. He began searching the night rooms, and hidden at the back of one of the bathroom wardrobes he found a black bag which contained some of the contraceptive devices that had been described in Stopes book.

"You crafty bitch" he muttered to himself. "I'll get you for this."

He took the bag, wrapped it in some waste paper and asked one of the servants to dispose of it. Then he settled down with a large brandy and waited for Olive to come home from the stables. Not long after she came to the drawing room adjacent to their bedroom, in flushed with youth and looking so radiant, her beauty would have stopped half the traffic in London if it had not been dark.

Henry saw none of the beauty that everyone else saw. All he saw was the woman he had been married to for almost ten years. He had come to notice every imperfection about her. Hardly a week went by when he did not notice something else that he did not like about her. She was like a ship which with every new storm lost some more of its paintwork, or picked up some more barnacles below the waterline. She was no rusty hull, but she was no longer the innocent girl he thought he had married.

"Hello" she shouted from across the room. Olive had never been innocent. Her life had been marked by moments that had made a notable impact on her. The first time she was whipped by Brooky. The day her mother brought Arthur home. Jack and the cottage children. The time Diarmid Wellesley nearly pushed her face in the fire. Mangerton Mountain and the episode with Shaun Riley. The night in Piccadilly Fountain. The loss of her virginity. Yet, she was still happy to see the husband, for she believed in marriage lasting forever, and rushed across the room towards him. "How is my wonderful Keddy tonight!" She threw herself into his lap and kissed him on the lips.

"Oh your Keddy is just fine" he replied. Keddy was his middle name, and many of his closest friends, including Eric, occasionally called him by it. Henry had lots of friends, but Olive had met very few of them over the years. The old idea that a woman's place was in the home was still prevalent amongst Henry's set, and he usually met his old schoolmates or college chums at the various clubs he was a member of.

"I am glad to find you home" Olive admitted into his ear "you are always out somewhere or the other."

"I was thinking the same about you."

"How is that?" she answered. "I was beginning to think you were avoiding me."

Henry laughed. It was one of those little laughs someone gives out when they think someone is lying to them. "That's a bit rich."

Olive sensed something was in the air. "Have I done something wrong?" She pulled her herself up and folded her arms.

"I didn't say that"

"What's your brother been saying now?" She was angry. Eric's rumours filtered back to her too. She had stopped going places with Jane in public, and spent more and more time at the stables.

"Don't you think it's strange that in all the time we've been married you've never got pregnant?" He had never brought the matter up before.

"No" said Olive.

"No?" quizzed Henry with some surprise.

"I did not think you wanted any children. Eric told me ..." She stopped. It was before she had even met Henry and was dating Eric. He had told her that Henry had a phobia about children, that he could not stand the sight of them. That had always stuck in her mind, and at sixteen she felt relieved that she would not be pressured into having children. Now, ten years later, it was a different story.

"Eric?" Henry asked expectantly.

"You hate children, yes?" Olive asked.

"No" Henry answered.

Olive was angry. She got up and lit a cigarette. How could she have been so stupid? She had lived all that time with Henry and the subject of children had never arisen. She had always assumed that he wanted none.

"Are you telling me that you want to have children?"

"Yes" he said without too much consideration.

"Jesus" Olive exploded in a sigh of relieve "All these years I have been avoiding pregnancy, I need not have? Is that what your saying?"

"I didn't even know you could have children," Henry uttered rather foolishly.

"There is absolutely nothing wrong with me, Keddy Fletcher. My doctor has told me endless times that I am built to be a baby machine."

"Oh." That was all Henry could muster in reply. "I didn't know."

Olive stared at him. He was an utter stranger to her. How could she live with someone so long and know so little about him. At the beginning of their marriage he had been forceful and energetic, but now he seemed weak and lacking in enthusiasm for life. Too many things had passed him by. Sure, he had a wonderful lifestyle, four homes, and oodles of money he did not know what to do with, but as a man, he was a bore, which he should not have been, for money buys power and influence, and any man with both is usually not dull. But dull was what Henry had become. If he took Olive out, then it was to the Covent Garden opera house, or the Shaftsbury Theatre, or some other boring venue full of stuffy people with stuffy throats and stuffed pockets. He never took her anywhere new. These places she had to find for herself, like the cinema and the films of Pickford, Fairbanks and Chaplin. It had not sunk in with Henry that the world had changed, that women had won the vote, and had their first woman member of Parliament. There was the Original Dixieland Jazz Band playing at the Palladium and bringing the house down, while Henry was at home thinking they were still living in the time of *Shine On Harvest Moon*.

"Sometimes you are such a fuddy-duddy, Keddy."

"What's a fuddy-duddy?" he asked.

"Someone who is a prig but is too old to know it."

Henry felt cut, but he had become used to cheap jibes by Olive about his age.

"Then I better not dilly-dally along the way then" he said mockingly. He tried to get up out of his chair, but Olive pushed him back and sat astride his knees. He tried to shake her off, but she would not budge.

"I would be forever blowing bubbles if you did" Olive countered. She was well into music and the arts. She had met many dancers and actresses, and was attracted by the lifestyle, the comradeship, but more than anything she fancied the idea of being a movie star. Mary Pickford was her idol;

she made acting look so simple. People had told Olive that she had the looks to be a star too, and she had come to believe them. She had taken up acting with a London amateur dramatic society which Henry was furious about.

"You've become a right bitch, did you know that? Ever since you started swanning around with those theatre low lives. Why can't you be like other women and have children?"

Olive had heard his arguments about her theatre associates before, but the plea for children was totally new. "I have always been a bitch, Keddy," she said with a puff of smoke. "Are you sure that's not what you'd get if you had children by me?"

"Who else am I going to have children by?" She exasperated him in a way that nobody else had ever been able to do, not even Eric.

"But you know I want to get into the movie business. Having children right now would put my career on hold."

"What career!" Henry was angry now. "You're my bloody wife, that's your career." As soon as he had said it he regretted it. It was not the way to go about getting what he wanted. He modified his tone. "Look, we'll do a deal. You have a couple of children, then I'll back you all the way to be a star, or whatever you call it."

Olive's face lit up. "You promise? You are not just saying that? You'll let me take real acting roles?"

"Yes." He saw how happy it made her and realised he had underestimated her determination to be an actress. She was extremely attractive, and just as pretty as Mary Pickford.

"Oh, darling" Olive purred sliding down his legs and into his arms "you should not get angry with me. Of course I want children, but I also do not want to end up fat and wrinkled by the time I'm thirty. I want to act because I think I am good at it. Chloe and I used to put on little plays for mama when we were young, and you know that my grandma Olive was an opera star in Vienna. It's in my blood, and there is nothing I can do about it, I must go with the flow."

She was playing with one of the little tufts of hair on the side of his head. She had him wrapped around her little finger like his hair. She was in control of their relationship. After years of appearing subservient to him, she no longer hid her single-mindedness. He could not clip her wings. She was like her grandmother Vivian, prone to attacks of temper, and extremely able at getting her own way. Henry was ill equipped to deal with her. The only way that he could keep her interest was by spoiling her, giving into her demands, and by constantly upping her allowance. It appeared that much of the wealth that had been acquired by robbing Marion Trainor, was being squandered by Olive on clothes, furnishings for the houses, lavish dinner parties, horses, and motor cars.

"Do you think you can afford children, Keddy?" she impudently asked him.

"No ... we'll have to sell your horses."

She laughed, for she thought he was joking, but Henry was quite serious. He had to make cuts in spending somewhere, for it was going out faster than it was coming in.

"Why don't you sell the run-down estate in Scotland instead" she smiled playfully, tickling him in the ribs. Henry thought she was playing with him, but she was quite serious.

"We'll see. Let's have the children first."

He slid his hand up beneath the lightweight material of her Paris fashion dress.

"Oh, wait a minute, darling" she trilled "Let me take my pearls off first." She removed her necklace and pushed the top of her dress down over her shoulders. She wore no undergarment, and the removal of her dress exposed her naked breasts. "Ouch" she let out as he drew one of her nipples into his mouth "Be gentle with me."

"They seem much bigger than usual" Henry retorted as he let her wet nipple slide off his tongue.

"Do they?" she teased as she pushed his head against her breasts again. She held him there while she felt his hand run up the inside of her dress and fumble at the opening of her drawers. "That's because I'm three months pregnant," she declared.

Henry's hand froze. He raised his head out of her breasts. "What did you say?"

Olive rose from his lap without replying and crossed the room in the direction of the bathroom. "I'm expecting in October" she turned, lingering at the bathroom door "but that does not mean that we cannot have sex."

She blew a kiss to Henry, and disappeared into the bathroom, leaving the door slightly ajar. It was obvious she wanted him to follow her, and of course, Henry could not stop himself from doing so, for once the initial shock had passed, he had to know if it was just another one of her teases that had always made her so irresistible, or was the plain truth.

PART TWO

1

It happened one summer's evening on the road to Brighton. Olive pulled her Vauxhall in at one of the new garages that had sprung up beside the road on the edge of London. She was alone. Their nanny in Belgrave Square was caring for the children and she had decided to spend the weekend on her own at the house in Brighton.

It had been a busy season. She had got back from the Riviera in early April in time for the new season. She and Henry had been going down to the South of France for the last four winters where he had often left her with Patricia and Barbara, their young daughters, while he returned to England on business. They usually roomed in the Grand Hotel du Cap d'Antibes near Cannes, took an apartment on the Cote de L'Esterel at St. Tropez, or stayed in Monte Carlo depending upon their mood, though Henry did not like to leave Olive on her own in Monte Carlo in case she developed a taste for *chemin de fer*. So more often than not, Olive found herself abandoned in St. Tropez when Henry had to return to London, though if Olive had been given the choice, she would have remained at the Grand on the Cote d'Azur.

There was nothing wrong with her four-litre seventy-five horsepower Vauxhall that could speed at seventy-five miles an hour. Henry had more or less gifted her the car after her first drive of it in Deauville. She wanted to fill it up the tank for the weekend, and when she pulled in, she noticed that the attendant had his head stuck under the bonnet of an Austro-Daimler, a large sports car like her own. She recognised the car type from watching the races at Brooklands, where friends and acquaintances raced every weekend. On weekday afternoons, for five shillings, anyone could pay to use the track and go at whatever speed they liked. Olive had done so many times and had fallen in love with its irregular shape, its several miles, and its steep banks. She had regularly taken part in the one-hour 'blind' races that were all about seeing who could travel furthest in that time. Outside of England, France was the only other country that had the means to indulge in the racing of sports cars.

It was with some interest that Olive got out of her car to look at the Austro-Daimler. The attendant still had his head stuck under the hood.

"Excuse me" she shouted out from a matter of a few feet " but is that ...."

She never finished her sentence. What stopped her was the sudden appearance of a brown-haired head from the depths of the Austro-Daimler. He was so good looking that it took her breath away. He was the first man that she had seen to rival the looks of poor dead Rupert Brooke. He had gorgeous blue eyes, was clean-shaven, and was about her own age, pushing thirty.

"Oh, sorry, didn't hear you drive in" he said in a plumy accent. "How can I help you, Miss?"

She was lost for words. She pointed to her car.

The attendant looked at the Vauxhall. "Nice car. It's the new Thirty Ninely-Eight, isn't it?" Then he began looking around as if he was searching for somebody else. "Where's your driver?"

Olive pouted her lips and gave him a long stare, at the same time tapping the side of her leg gently with one of her driving gloves. He was just like all the men she had ever met. They seemed to think that because women over thirty had the vote that they would stay in the kitchen and tend the children. She was six months under thirty, and she was unhappy that men over twenty-one could vote while she could not. Yet, she could not be angry with him for his mistake; he was too handsome, and she used the opportunity to gaze at him without embarrassment.

"Oh, sorry" he stammered as he realised his mistake. A look of curiosity filled is face as he looked to the car and then back to Olive again. "Sorry" he repeated.

"Could you fill her up, please" Olive she said brusquely. She had the upper hand again. The pleasure of his good looks had given away to the reality that he was just a garage attendant. Whatever fantasies she had of him being another Rupert Brooke quickly evaporated.

"Where are you off to?" he asked as he poured in the petrol.

"Brighton" she replied. She thought not to say anything else, but she could not stop herself. Despite herself, there was something about him that excited her. "For the weekend. I have a house there."

"Oh" said the attendant "I live in Kent. I'm just down here for the weekend." He pointed to the car. "Race her at Brooklands most weekends if I'm not in France. Thought I'd have a rest for once."

This time it was Olive's turn to say "Oh ....." He was not a garage attendant all the time he was a racing driver. "Do you make money from it?"

"Certainly do" He had emptied one can of petrol into the Vauxhall, and had stopped to pick up a second. Olive took a quick furtive glance at his bottom as he bent. It was lovely. "I make money racing in France too. I've got an Amilcar stored at Cannes."

"Really" Olive exclaimed. "I'm not long back from the South of France. Have you met the Fletchers?" She was probing to see if he knew her husband.

"Don't mix much social apart from old college and war chums. I was in the Royal Flying Corps before it came the Royal Air Force. After one's been up in a plane bombing the hell out of the Hun, a race in a fast car is the next best thing."

The War had re-shaped everyone's lives, and scarred it too. "Did you know Reggie Warneford?" she asked.

"He bought it a couple of years before I came down from Cambridge. Sorry." He said it in such a way that sounded totally genuine. But he had let slip his age. Olive placed him as being about three years younger than her. "I bought this garage after the War, more a hobby than anything." He was so intent in his conversation with Olive, petrol began to pour out of the tank." I say! Sorry, about that!"

"Not to worry" Olive smiled feeling the urge to touch him, but instead hoping from one foot to the other, waving her hands about, and feeling like a clown. In his presence she felt completely awkward. "What is your name?" she asked, as he replaced the petrol cap.

"Tony .... well, really it's Wilfred Joynson Wreford, but everyone calls me Tony, it's much friendlier."

"Pleased to meet you, Tony" She held out her hand. "My name's Olive." Suddenly she noticed she had offered her hand that still had a glove on. She pulled her hand back, removed the glove, and offered her hand again. He meanwhile had wiped his hand on his overalls, and as he took her hand, she felt the warmth of his being, and the strength of his character. It was the hand of a playboy which had held a tennis racket as often as machine wrench, but at that moment, his fingernails were ingrained with oil, and his palm lubricated by grease. He made no excuse about it.

She settled her bill for the petrol with him, he opened the driver's door for her, and closed it behind her once she was seated.

"Will you be at Brooklands next weekend" she asked him. "I go there a lot to watch the races."

"No" he replied "I'll be back over in France to prepare for Le Mans and the Bol d'Or." Olive was disappointed. "However, I will be in Brighton tomorrow evening if you would like to have dinner?"

Olive knew she had to decline, but she didn't. "The Royal Albion at seven?" she suggested impulsively.

"It's a deal!" He stepped up on to the running board and kissed her on the cheek.

Olive blushed. She started the car to hide her embarrassment, and with a little wave to Tony, she looked over her shoulder, and pulled out on to the Brighton road not knowing what she had done or where it would lead.

Henry and Olive sat through the ladies final at Wimbledon hardly saying a word to one another. They watched Suzanne Lenglen win an unprecedented fifth title in a row, and at the end of it, all Henry could say was "I'm glad that's over."

On the short journey back to their apartment at Grosvenor House, Olive sat in the back of their chauffeur driven Silver Ghost, hoping Henry would not ask her any more questions.

"Nobody goes to the Cote d'Azur between March and October. What's got into you? Why do you want to go and lie in the sun?"

"It's the fashion, Henry. You are just too old to understand anything."

As the years went by, the twenty-three years that separated them had become a gulf.

"I think you've got infatuated with someone again. Tell me straight. You've been like this before. Who is it this time?"

After the birth of the children, Olive had been seen with a number of men, but nothing had ever happened. It had been, as Henry said, a series of infatuations that had soon passed. "It's got nothing to do with anybody else, Keddy. It's you. I need a break from you. I want to get away for from you for awhile to be on my own. Can you not understand that? I've done everything you've ever asked of me, and now I want to do something for myself."

Henry had no means of countering her attack on him. Maybe a break in the south of France was what was needed. He was sick of having to be seen with a wife who was curt with him. He loved her dearly, but he certainly managed to live a happier life when she was not about. He did not want to lose her entirely, but he knew he would if he did not give her more slack.

"When will you back?" he asked.

"When I feel like it," she snapped.

Nothing more was said between them. They had guests coming for dinner, and afterwards Olive was in bed before Henry finally saw his old cronies off at the door. He woke her and tried to make love to her, but she became angry and pushed him away. The rest of the night he spent in a halfway state between sleep and consciousness, thinking about his life, where he had gone wrong, and how the children would cope while their mother was away in France.

*

Tony Wreford, ex-war pilot and racing driver, was not all that he first seemed. There were two things he failed to tell Olive

Fletcher, before and after he had bedded her in Brighton. The first he should have told her about right away - he was married.

The twenty-four hour race at Le Mans had gone well enough for him and Jim Mollison, a chum from his old squadron, except that the car had broken down after seventeen hours and thirteen minutes. They were well and truly out of the money, and Jim had to get back to his commercial flying job with Imperial Airways. Tony was left with the headache of fixing the car and getting back across the Channel to his playboy pursuits, but a chance meeting with another old war chum at the Hotel Lotti in Paris took him to Le Touquet where he won a few thousand pounds in the Casino.

Tony was on a roll. What was the point of going back to his wife Frances and their apartment with the Joynson Hicks at Plaistow Hall, Kent, when she had her own money anyway? He could extend his stay in France for a couple of months, doing the racing circuits, and the tables. So he lingered on at Le Tourquet, then Deauville, which since the war had become a popular resort for the Bright Young Things from London.

The English, according to Tony, had always been ambivalent about going abroad. Despite their longing for an escape to lands where the sun shone all day, they had a mistrust of the unsanitary and unpredictable manners that foreigners seemed to possess. On the one hand was the allure of warm blue seas and rivers of wine, while on the other, indigestible food and people by misfortune not born English. This was the sort of English person he found in Le Tourquet and Deauville, places that since the end of the war had been so overrun by the English that they had begun to look like Eastbourne and Brighton.

Tony wanted something else. Although he had been to Cannes many times - he had his Amilcar garaged there - he had never done the season on the Riviera, but he knew that out of season, the coast was deserted and that apartments were cheap. Besides, it did not make sense to hang around the Channel, his wife might want to come over and that would spoil everything. So he packed the Austro-Daimler with a few hangers-on he picked up in Deauville and drove to the Cote d' Azur, stopping to take in a few races, and wagers, on the way.

*

When Olive arrived at the Cap d' Antibes, she did not have the Grand Hotel to herself, as she believed she might. The Americans had moved in, and the dining room and tables were full of their light, frivolous talk. It had never dawned on Olive that when the English went home to enjoy spring and summer that the Americans descended on Cannes to lie on the beaches. Although she knew her way around the shops and restaurants of the Cote d' Azur, she knew nothing of the beaches; it was all new to her. Yet, more exceptionally, the scenery was much more spectacular in the summer than it was in the winter. The brilliant blue sea gave a welcomed cool from the heat rather than a shivering chill, and the scent of lemon, orange, pine, and eucalyptus was far more aromatic. Everywhere seemed to be alive, while in all her previous visits, there had always seemed to be a cold stiffness and unbreakable formality to every little thing. It was then that it dawned on her that the liveliness and joie d'vivre was emanating from the objects that made Antibes in the summer so significantly richer in appeal - the Americans.

Olive had got nowhere with her acting career. Jane Warneford-Cooper had managed to get herself a part in the silent movie The Virgin Queen, but Olive had not been successful at all. Jane had tried to get her the right introductions, but unlike Jane who was widow, the things expected of her meant compromising her marriage. Yes, she had pursued a number of men, her infatuations as Henry called them, but it had been with the purpose of furthering her acting career. Nothing had come of it except acute embarrassment when she had not allowed herself to be seduced. As a result, the private singing, dancing, and acting lessons she had been taking, had all been a waste of time.

This personal failure had depressed her. She had excelled best at dance, and the constant removal to the Riviera every winter had also broken her chances to get a part in a West End revue, for she had been called for auditions three times, but on each occasion she had been stuck in Saint Tropez with the children. This time she would not isolate herself on the Cote de

L'Esterel, even if Tony Wreford suggested it to avoid gossip.

Where was Tony? His telegram stated that he would be at the station to meet her when she arrived off the Blue Train, but he had not. After checking into the hotel she expected to be buzzed to say that he had arrived, but he did not. In fact a whole week passed and she heard nothing from him. It had been his idea that she should join him in the Riviera, an indication that the week-long affair they had enjoyed before his departure for France had been meaningful. It had injected life into her. Their lovemaking had been wild; he was only the second man to have entered her, and she treated the matter seriously. After that first evening in Brighton when they had taken dinner and she had gone to his hotel room and spent the night with him, she had decided to leave Henry. Tony had made her realise all the things she had missed by marrying at the age of sixteen. She needed love, strong physical love that made her feel like a woman, not a society wife with obligations and duties that reflected the importance of her husband. She had no idea how much she had lost herself by being Mrs. Henry Fletcher. Whatever had happened to Olive Trainor? The young girl from Teddington with Irish parents? Where had she gone?

She had been persuaded by Tony to stay on at Brighton through the weekend to the Wednesday of the following week, during which they hardly ever got out of bed. They made love so many times, she became sore from sex, a new and invigorating experience, that made her crave for more. His penis was much larger than Henry's, and his movements much swifter. He could lift her clear of the floor and make love to her while standing. It was at the climax of one such session that she decided that Henry was history and that she would divorce him.

Now, waiting in the Hotel Grand du Cap, and one week gone, she thought it more prudent to wait awhile before announcing to Henry her intentions. In England she had dreamt of meeting Tony in Antibes, making love, then sending Henry a telegram saying that it was all over. However, during the train journey, it had occurred to her that Henry might try to cut her off financially and then delay settlement for years. No, it would be better if she wrote to him asking for a trail separation until she could come to terms with her depression. No, that was not right either, it sounded as though she was mentally ill. In the end she concluded that the best thing to do for the present was to string Henry along until she had a real reason to leave him - a firm commitment from Tony that he wanted to marry her.

All that seemed pie in the sky after a week at the hotel. She spent every moment of the day looking for him, imagining what had delayed him, scanning the beach, being chauffeured up and down the coast looking for his car, leaving notes for him at the desk when she went to look for him. In all it was the actions of someone in love, someone who had been charmed, seduced, and infatuated with her seducer. It made her a bag of nerves. Had he just used her for sex? Had some accident occurred to him? Had she scared him off by agreeing to come? She thought of everything, but she woke up every morning with the belief that he would arrive that day, and went to bed late every night with the belief he would arrive the following day.

Olive became so wrapped up in her thoughts for Tony, that some of the other guests began to notice the beautiful white skinned Englishwoman sitting day after day on her own. They nicknamed her the 'White Lady'.

"How's the White Lady today then" some American guest would ask with a jerk of his head. "Prince Charming shown up in his white horse yet?"

"Nope, not yet" someone would reply.

"Heh, maybe it's me" some wise guy would joke.

There were plenty of contenders. No one in the Grand was ugly, ill nourished, and devoid of intelligence. None of them were vermin ridden, cold, and hungry living in a dirty hotel in a strange land like tossed driftwood, to be thrown like debris to their deaths. They were all rich Americans. They were individuals, not some types, for types were nothing, types were not worth knowing. No one who came to the Grand de Cap was a type.

Into the midst of all this, walked Zelda and Scott Fitzgerald. We must mention Zelda first, for it was she that everyone noticed long before they noticed Scott. They were both under thirty and at the height of their confidence and powers. These were the powers of creation; to make a contemporary world that everyone wanted to be part of. They began coming to The Grand in the evening from their villa at St. Raphael. They were bored; they were looking for ways to kill the cancer of conformity. They were inseparable. Some look would come over them as they entered the Grand, as if they were waiting for something to happen; as if they seemed to be looking forward to something fantastic. Something had to happen, something extravagant, and every night from the first evening they entered, something would. Zelda would dance alone and raise her skirts above her waist, swaying rhythmically to the hotel orchestra. Speeches were made, and toasts drunk. Zelda would leap on to a chair, take off her panties and throw them at whatever man she liked. She was an exhibitionist, but she was also destructive. She challenged Scott to diving games off the rocks at night, thirty feet above the water, their timing saving them from the rocks below. One evening on the terrace she had come along and plunked down right beside Olive without an introduction.

"They don't seem to understand that I am not trying to get anything - at least I don't think I am - but to get rid of some of myself."

She sat long enough in one place to light a cigarette. She looked over her shoulder, as if she was expecting to be called any minute, and then blew some smoke into the air. She was drunk.

"Women go through life with a death-bed air, either snatching the last moment, or with the resignation of a martyr. I'm the first. You're the latter. I can tell" Zelda pointed at Olive with her cigarette hand "you're the kind of girl who's gonna tell me how misunderstood she is. Look, you're already straightening out your skirt as proof that you'll make a good mother! Admit it, you're the kind of girl that'll tell me that she doesn't mind the number of cigarettes I smoke, but you'll count them just the same, and tell me I'm killing myself."

Zelda had brought her own glass with her. She drained it. "See, a girl like me and a dull girl like you have nothing to say to each other. That's why I can only talk to men." She stubbed her cigarette on the terrace stone. "Scott and I hate women." She got up and went back to the bar.

Zelda and Scott were only part of the individuality of the Americans that surrounded Olive as she waited for Tony. Ernest Hemingway hung out the bar scribbling; Cole Porter hid himself in his room; while Valentino rushed in one afternoon and left the next. Middle-aged dancer Isadora Duncan went about bare-footed and tête-à-tête with her young Russian lover who spent all his time composing poetry for her.

Most notably, what separated Olive from the other guests was her whiteness. While they gathered on Eden Roc or went down to the sands, Olive continued to watch for Tony from the shade of the terrace or the awnings by the pool, until even she became exasperated with the experience. It was Isadora Duncan who rescued her.

"Why don't you come with us, duchess" she called her on the morning following the Zelda episode. "We're going to look for a piece of land to build our villa. Then we're going over to the Carlton for luncheon to get away from the flappers." It was obvious from her tone she meant Zelda Fitzgerald. "This is the place to be in summer, isn't it? Who wants to fry in L.A."

Olive could not stand the waiting anymore. She had passed ten days in abject misery. As usual, she told the concierge where she could be found if a certain young gentleman was looking for her.

"The bastards are all the same!" Isadora shouted as they roared alone the coastal road. "They promise you a goldmine, get you into bed, get their rocks off, and you never see the bastards again." Olive had never heard anyone use such language before, and she was wondering if she was alluding to Tony. "Between you and me, duchess, men are only good for one thing - walking on, because that's exactly what they do to us."

"Oh, but I'm married" said Olive trying to cover her reason for being there.

"What's that got to do with it? Life's too short to tie yourself to somebody who'll use you like a doormat. Believe me, I know, I've done it three times already."

"Married three times?"

"Lived with men as their wife!" she corrected. "Four if you count Rasputin here." She pointed to the front of the car. "He's the first one I've married. The best thing about him" she stated in a lower tone "is his dick ..." she nudged "and his poetry of course."

Olive tried to appear as if the conversation was the type of thing she was used to. She felt that Isadora was about to ask her about her own sexual life.

"Do you have any children?" Olive asked in an attempt to change the subject.

Isadora came over pale then regained her composure. "I lost my children ten years ago ... by drowning." Her eyes strayed out across the blue Med. "They were being driven home after having lunch with me in Paris when the car stalled on a hill. The chauffeur got out to restart the engine while the children and Nanny remained in the back. Suddenly, the car began running backwards down the hill and plunged into the Seine. Deirdre was seven, and Patrick was five."

Olive reached across and put her hand on Isadora's hands that had come to rest in her lap. "I'm sorry," she said. She understood what it felt like to have two children. To be separated from them was one thing, but to lose them entirely, and so tragically, the thought was unbearable.

"Do you have children?" the dancer asked recovering from her gloom.

"Yes" Olive was pleased to announce "Two girls. Patricia is four, and Barbara two and a half."

"Don't you miss them?" Isadora quizzed.

Until that moment Olive had not missed her children. She had spent all her time thinking about Tony without once being worried about them. As far as she was concerned they were in good hands with their Nanny. Henry doted on them so much, if anything they would be spoiled rather than neglected. She always thought of them as Henry's children, not her own. Why this was so she did not know, but something in her made her feel that they belonged to him, that he deserved them, that if she wanted, she could have more for herself while he could not.

"Of course I miss them" she lied. She did not sound very convincing.

"How old are you, duchess?"

Olive was reluctant to answer such a question. She would be thirty in two-months time. Tony was almost three years her junior, and she felt it looked bad waiting for a younger man.

"I'm twenty six" she replied "twenty seven in September."

"My god" Isadora exclaimed "I'm forty-six. I've got twenty years on you. You've got the whole world ahead of you. Now tell me, duchess, why do you sit in the Grand all day looking like a boiled fish? The place is full of gorgeous men."

Olive laughed. It was the first time she had laughed for weeks. The anxiety and tension of leaving Henry in London to be with Tony had made her clam up. Suddenly she felt like opening up to Isadora and told her brief life story, including her desire to be a stage performer, particularly a dancer.

"Je le connais!" Isadora exclaimed "You want to be a star like moi!"

It had not dawned on Olive that perhaps Isadora could help her get a foot on the stage.

"Do you think it is possible?" Olive asked

"Tout es possiblé." She had suddenly lapsed into French, as if talk of the arts and her profession called for a different kind of Isadora Duncan. "All children dance, but who is a dancer? Fear of our own inabilities. That is what limits us most. The biggest difference in the world is between the amateur and the professional. She who does not name herself as a practitioner - and She who is paid for it and defines herself by her work. To become a dancer you must first call yourself a dancer. It is the same in all the arts. Comprise? So, I'll ask you the question everyone will ask you - what do you do?"

Isadora was holding open a door for her. Until that moment she had never thought of herself as a dancer, but as the wife of Henry Fletcher. Convention had dictated that she took on her husband's name, a subsuming of her female identity. She had only now begun to play with the idea that her marriage to Henry should have been a partnership of equals. She was not going to be Zelda Fitzgerald's woman of martyred resignation, her life dulled and destroyed by motherhood, straightening the creases in her skirt as her mother Marion had done. Her mother's beauty had passed away into a bag of lines by the time she was forty, ugly cruel looking lines that had sapped every ounce of her fine features from her. Olive could feel her own beauty being drained from her by Henry and her children. She had nothing to say to them in the way that Zelda had nothing to say to her.

"I am a dancer" Olive answered Isadora. It was a moment she would never forget.

Isadora was pleased that she had another convert. "Do have a stage name?"

"Trainor" announced Olive thinking of her maiden name.

"No, no" tutted Isadora. "Sound's like an army exercise instructor. You need something more like my own ... half man, half woman." Isadora's real name was Angela Duncan.

They ran through a number of names and finally settled on Trevor.

"Olive Trevor" Isadora said in a French accent. "Perfectament! We'll audition you at the Grand later. Mon Dieu, Rasputin! Let's get there alive!"

All the while Rasputin (Olive did not discover his real name) had been driving them at neck break speed along the road to Cannes. The road twisted and turned and there was a distinct smell of burning rubber.

"Stop! Stop!" shouted Isadora.

Rasputin pulled the car up with a screech and a cloud of dust that left them perched on the side of a cliff.

"This is the spot! This is where I want my villa!" She jumped out of the car and ran to the edge. "See, there is just enough space to have a garden and a swimming pool as well. Gregori! Gregori!" she called Rasputin. He got out of the car and went to her side. She pointed to the place she envisaged the villa to be built. "Isn't it beautiful." She made her husband kiss her, then turned her back on him, while he thrust his hands on to her breasts. Slowly he moved them down her body to her panty-line while she rubbed her buttocks against his inner thighs. She undid the belt of his trousers and plunged one of her hands down between his legs to take hold of his manhood. In equally quick time, having pulled up the hem of her short dress, he pushed his long brown fingers up inside her.

Olive had to look away. She sank into the back seat of the car and waited. From where she lounged she could see the twin domes of the Carlton. It was said they were modelled on a famous beauty who had died earlier that Spring.

"Didn't that Sarah Bernhardt have a great pair of tits" Isadora declared pointing to the domes as she got back into the car five minutes later. Her own breasts were large and popping out of her blouse, their long nipples pushing through the flimsy material, still erect from Gregori fondling them.

"Drive us to the Carlton, Gregori, it's time for dejeuner."

Gregori smiled and did what he was told. She turned to sit next to Olive smelling of sex. "Gregori's grandfather was a Count, but he's a true Bolshevik like me. Viva La Revolution! Long live Lenin!"

The troubles in Russia meant nothing to

Olive even though her husband had helped the Whites, and her maternal grandfather and grandmother had been Russian. Politics was not her concern. She knew events in Russia had an influence on workers and that was why there was unrest in the factories and mines across Europe. Why Isadora should become involved in such things was beyond Olive, it did not make sense.

"My god!" shouted Isadora as they pulled up in front of the Carlton. She grabbed Olive by the wrist. "This may be your lucky day. It's Andre Charlot. Andre! Andre!" she called to a man of Olive's age wearing spectacles.

Olive did not have a clue who Andre Charlot was, but from the look on his face, he was not overwhelmed at being recognised by the infamous Isadora Duncan. "Izzy!" he shouted back. Gregori gave Olive a weary look, for it was obvious he was having a hard time keeping up with the past of his wife.

Andre took Isadora's hand and helped her out of the car. She hugged and kissed him passionately, much to the annoyance of Gregori, then introduced Gregori and Olive to him. They went hand in hand into the hotel, Gregori and Olive tagging on behind like a pair of puppy dogs.

*

Tony Wreford had overplayed his hand. After telegramming Olive Fletcher to join him at Cannes, he received another telegram from his wife saying that she was bored in London and was coming down to Cannes to be with him. She had arrived three days before Olive checked-in, and in that time, they had managed to reconcile their marriage which had been under strain for some time.

Frances Agnes Wreford was the same age as Tony. They had known each other since they were children in Exeter, as she was the daughter of his father's best friend. Even when Tony had left The Firs and gone up to Dean Close School, Gloucester to join his brother Bertrand, he still saw her during the vacations. There was no romance between them in those days, they were just good friends. Then when the War broke in '14, Tony went up to Pembroke College, Cambridge to join his brother, but Bertrand gave up his studies and transferred to the Royal Military College at Camberley. By November he was a second lieutenant in the Devon Regiment; the following April he was killed at Ypres. This brought nineteen year old Tony and Frances closer together and they had married in the winter of '15.

Frances and Tony had known each other so long that they knew everything about each other. They could not keep secrets from one other, and it soon came out that Tony had seduced a Mrs. Fletcher and now she was chasing after him.

"There's nothing serious in this, is there?" she asked.

"Nothing, flower ... it was just one of those things. I slept with her and she gets the wrong idea. I mean, it's the twenties ... nothing's for keeps nowadays." He turned his nose up. "When one's been through a war and come out the other side, one realises what a miracle it is that one's still alive." He liked to play the suffering hero when it suited him.

Frances had strayed at times too. They had both taken lovers over the years but had always returned to one another. It was as if they knew that nothing could really become between them.

"You're not going to see her, are you? I'll cut your balls off if you do," she said after three days when he told her that he was supposed to meet Olive at the station that afternoon.

"Of course not. The woman's infatuated with me. God knows what she would do if she found out you were here. Anyway, she's booked in at the Grand. The chances of her coming over to the Carlton and us running into to her are a million to one. You know the two sets don't mix."

"Why don't we go for a spin then, just in case?" Frances suggested. "You can drive me up to Grasse and buy me some perfume."

"What do we want to go there for? Can't we give it a miss and drive on to Monte."

"We can do both. We might pick up a Renoir someone's missed. Or a Matisse we could sell to the Stein's" she compromised. She was in the process of talking Picasso into doing a painting for her. She had run into him on Golfe Juan a couple of times. She did not want to run into a furious Mrs. Fletcher. "Let's stay overnight too."

Thus, Frances kept Tony busy doing this

and that, going here and there, passing time like the idle rich only knew how, for they had no work to go to, and thus no work to do. Their sole raison d'etre was the pursuit of pleasure, but the Wreford's did not have a limitless supply of cash. They did have to work; they had to find ways of making money at the tables, by racing Tony's car, by using Frances as a lure for wagers. She knew a bit about modern art and dabbled in buying and selling. They were in the modern sense of the word hustlers, people who had no profession but who were professional about looking for opportunities. There was also a hidden income, regular payments of cash authorised by Tony's second cousin Sir Willam Joynson Hicks, secretary to the Treasury, and a member of Baldwin's cabinet. The money came by a circuitous route, and in return Tony had to wire back specific information. There were a large number of Russian émigrés dislodged by the revolution already living in the south of France, and it was information on these individuals that he was asked to supply most. The communists had lodged their own spies amongst them, and it was well known that the Hotel Cap d' Eden Roc was their base. The British put their men into the Carlton, while the Americans preferred the Hotel de Cap d' Antibes.

He had forgotten all about Mrs. Fletcher by the time he was coming down the stairs at the Carlton on his way to a game of tennis. He was running late and convinced that his partner would not wait if he did not hurry.

Frances was down on the beach with some of the other wives, and Tony was eager to set up a wager with his American playing partner. That was all he had on his mind when he ran straight into Isadora Duncan's party.

"I beg your pardon" he said before he realised who was with them.

"Tony!" Olive declared in shock.

"Jesus, Olive ....." He had been in some jams but this was one of the worst he had ever found himself in. Even the time he had to shake Richthofen off his tail was nothing to this. Then he remembered that he had always lied about the Richthofen incident. The Red Baron had roasted to death three months before he had got to the front with the 21st Squadron. It was his fellow pilots who had nicknamed him Tony after he had rallied them during one dull afternoon with a rendition of Mark Antony's forum speech from Shakespeare's *Julius Caesar*. That was the closest he ever got to be a hero. Death was too real not be scared most of the time, but it was, as he realised, nothing compared to a woman's ire.

"Is that all you can say to me?" She slapped him across the face.

"Bravo!" shouted Isadora. "Anyone for tennis?"

"Olive, please ... meet me in an hour at your hotel?"

"So you can make a fool of me again? You can talk to me right here."

"What" he said startled "Right here in the lobby ... in front of them?"

"Yes!"

"Everyone will hear us. Can we not go somewhere private?"

"I've got nothing to hide" Suddenly Olive picked something up in his reaction. "But you have, haven't you? You've got some other bird-brain caged away upstairs singing like canary, haven't you?"

"We'll meet you in the dining room, duchess" Isadora interrupted.

"No, I'm coming with you. Goodbye, Mr. Wreford!" As she forced her way past him, she kicked him in the shin.

"Olive" he cried after her, but the situation was lost.

"We thought you were splendid, didn't we, boys" Isadora complimented her as they sat on the terrace eating.

"Not a friend of yours then, Miss Trevor?" Andre Charlot assumed. She had been introduced to Andre as Olive Trevor.

"I thought he was." She sat gloomily in her chair. Unfortunately, where they sat on the terrace overlooked the tennis courts. Tony Wreford was taking a thrashing.

"Looks as though you've put poor old Tony off his game, Olive. It's the first time I've seen him being knocked all over the court." Olive gaped at Isadora "You know him?"

"Of course we do. He's a notorious playboy. We know him from Paris. How about you Andre?"

"I met his wife on the beach an hour ago taking to some portrait painter."

Olive almost dropped her fork that had been hovering over a small bowl of fruit salad. The bastard was married. She felt cheated. Then she remembered that she too was married. What if he felt that it was all too complicated to work? What would she have done if Henry had joined her? For appearances, would she have cut off all contact with Tony? She supposed it made sense. With his wife in Cannes, he probably reacted the way any English person would for appearance sake. Tony would not risk meeting her for the fear of scandal. But why did he not send a note.

"What does all this matter!" exploded Gregori in a strong Russian accent. It was almost the first time that Olive had heard him speak. "This Tony is a parasite. In the Soviet Union he would be shot." Olive did not doubt it for a moment. The stories that had been coming out of the new Russia did not make it a place for a vacation. "What has happened here in the west? The War has changed nothing!"

"My dance schools have changed the way people look at dance," she suggested in an attempt to switch the focus of the conversation back to her. Isadora was proud of the schools she had opened in France, Germany, Russia, and the United States. "I saw Anna Pavlov doing the Dying Swan in Paris and I laughed. People laugh at my improvised movements on stage to master composers, so why cannot I laugh at the strictly defined movements of the great Pavlov and laugh. Take anyone to a ballet for the first time, and I guarantee they will laugh. It is only the po-faces of the deluding public who have paid fortunes to see art that prevents the world from laughing at the absurd antics of classical ballet."

"My darling, Isadora" Gregori interrupted "I cannot agree. My grandfather was a ballet and opera director in Russia and Vienna. He was a great artist. I am all for the free movement of the spirit, but this spirit must be shaped into form or it is not poetry."

"You can put poetry into form, but I refuse to have dance limited to chassé and pas de bourrée! The matter is at a close. I shall continue to dance and teach in my own inimitable way." She looked down to the tennis courts. "Perhaps Tony could do with some help with his footwork, eh Olive?"

Tony had just lost his footing and forfeited the match. He seemed to reach into the pocket of his shorts and grudgingly hand over some cash to his opponent. Olive, despite her anger with him, could not keep her eyes off him. He was a beautiful looking man.

"I've got Jack Buchanan debuting in my new Review on Broadway" Andre was divulging to Isadora. Olive was miles away recalling the time she had spent with Tony in Brighton. It had been real and she was convinced that he had fallen for her in a big way. She had to find out, and she owed it to him to give himself a chance to explain. As he began walking off the courts, she excused herself from the table.

"Don't be long, duchess. We'll be heading back soon" Isadora said with a wink.

"Alright" she replied and made her way to reception where she scribbled a note for Tony asking him to meet her that night at a small inn she had discovered at St. Paul-de-

Vence. She asked for the note to be handed to him personally.

Olive then waited discretely in one of the small lounges in the hope of catching sight of Mrs. Wreford, but Isadora and Gregori appeared not much longer afterwards and she went and joined them as they were about to leave.

"André took quite a shine to you, duchess" Isadora teased her "I told him that you were looking for a part in a revue and he said he would see what he could do. I think you are in."

Their car was brought to the front.

"Would you like to drive, Miss Trevor?" Gregori asked her.

"Would I just!" she exclaimed. It was red type eight cylinder Bugatti and ever since she had got to the Riviera, she had felt lost without a car. She missed her 30/98 Vauxhall dearly.

Isadora and Gregori settled themselves in the back of the car, and almost before Olive had moved off, they were fondling one another. She could see them in one of the wing mirrors but she shifted the angle of it so that she saw only the road. As they pulled out of the Carlton, Olive suddenly heard Isadora shout. "Bonjour, Madame Wreford!"

Olive could not look round as they passed by a small group of ladies, one of whom was strikingly beautiful and carrying a painting under her arm. It was the beautiful one that turned back her head slightly to reply "Bonjour!"

Olive had no doubt as she watched Frances

recede in the wing mirror, that if she wanted Tony Wreford for herself, she had a fight on her hands.

*

Henry Fletcher was wondering if his wife was ever going to come home. She had been away three months and he had received only one postcard. He began to worry that her state of mind was not everything it should be. The London season was coming to an end, and he was determined, for the sake of his marriage more than appearances, to find out why she had not come back. Naturally, he would take the children as they had done the previous four years, and go to the Riviera. The chauffeur would drive the Rolls down to St. Tropez, while he, the children, and the Nanny would go first class by train. Then, he changed his mind. If his wife did not want to communicate with him, then no news was good news. He would spend the winter in London and Brighton after all, and if she wanted to come home, he would be there for her as he had always been.

*

At this point in the story we must stop, for there is so much to tell, and little time to tell it in. Life moves at such a pace nowadays that often we find that we have neither the time nor the inclination to discover things about the past. True, the present is our immediate concern, and the future, if we are to contemplate such an idea, is such an uncertain thing that we prepare ourselves for it as best we can. But the past? How can we prepare ourselves to deal with our pasts?

There is a well worn saying that so often sounds like giving into fate, yet undeniably, at moments of truth, best describes a thing gone wrong 'One has made one's bed and one must lie in it.' Such an expression sounds as if it was coined to describe the behaviour of dogs, but as we know, it is employed to describe a thing that has gone wrong but which must be endured for better or worse.

In the case of Olive Fletcher and Tony Wreford, the thing that had gone wrong was their marriages. Therefore, you must not judge their folly, for who really knows what we are doing with our lives before we are forty? In our own times we see all around us the disintegration of relationships, the damage that separation brings, the sorrow that is reaped. But also, if we are truthful, we witness moments of sheer joy and are affected by the energy of young individuals released from the drudgery of their unhappy marriages. In the end, we might come down in judgement on friends who have separated and take sides in their parting, but in the case of Olive and Tony, let us not do so, let us remain open-minded, and believe that all would be well before war and plague, illness and madness descended upon them and destroyed their loving.

ROBBIE MOFFAT

The author was born and schooled in Glasgow. He took a degree in English language and Literature at Newcastle University. He began writing when he was seventeen and has a had a career as a poet, novelist, playwright and screenwriter. He is best known for his feature film work in which he is also a director and producer.

His prose writing as been overshadowed by this. He wrote his first novel when he was twenty two and continued to write novels for the next twenty years. None of them were published.

The rediscovery of his prose work has lead to a recent spate of publications that has lead to a resurgence of interest in his prose work.